MURDER IN THE LIBRARY

A WORD TRAVELS MOBILE BOOKSHOP COZY MYSTERY
BOOK 1

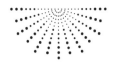

PENNY BROOKE

CHAPTER ONE

There's nothing I love more than the open road. When I'm driving with the music on full blast and the wind blowing through my hair, I feel free. After spending my twenties stuck behind a desk in a soulless corporate building, my life on the road feels like a dream.

"I don't understand this map," my aunt, Daisy Mae, said from the passenger seat. She was holding a massive map of the United States, squinting at it as if it had personally offended her. Aunt Daisy Mae was in her sixties, but her face didn't betray her age. She had very few fine lines, and her eyes were still alight with mischief. Lately she had been allowing her gray hair to grow out, but it only added to her disorganized artist appeal.

"That might have to do with the fact that you're looking for a teeny tiny route on a giant map of the entire country," I pointed out in amusement. I turned the music down as I spoke, since Aunt Daisy Mae always complained when I didn't. She had the unfortunate habit of talking loudly whenever a song got to the good part, then expected me to turn it down. It wasn't her best quality, but I would take all her worst qualities as long as she kept accompanying me on the road.

"Say what you want," Aunt Daisy Mae said, looking affronted, "but don't come running to me when we're lost. Are we close to Chicago?"

"Nowhere near it," I said with a shrug, causing her to groan and turn the map upside down. "We've done this trip a million times over the past two years. I know how to get to Greenwood. Trust me."

Aunt Daisy Mae let out a loud snort. "Trust you? That's what you said when we got lost in Arkansas, and look how that turned out!"

"You loved Arkansas," I reminded her gently. "Yeah, we got lost, but we sold a lot of books, and you even got that policeman's number. Remember?"

"Oh." A slow smile stretched across her face. "Right. I forgot about that. He had a great face but such a boring personality. He only ever wanted to talk about football. Or was that the guy in Little Rock?"

4

Aunt Daisy Mae shoved the map back into her handbag and put her feet on the dashboard before turning the music back up. I smiled and shook my head at her. She was such a character. Life would be extremely boring without her.

When I was laid off from my job a few years ago, I told my mother about my intention to buy an old van and turn it into a mobile bookstore. I had been a copy editor at one of the largest publishing houses in the country—LionHeart Publishing. I'd chosen a career that would keep me as close to books as possible, but the reality was that my job was painstakingly boring and exposed me to the impossible politics of the publishing world. Soon after starting the job, I realized that my real dream was to own a bookstore. Which was why I had been so excited to share my news with my mother. It had been a huge mistake. My mother called me in hysterics and told me that I was throwing my life away. She told me that I had to be more like my older brother, who had a house, wife, and three beautiful children. It was an uncomfortable conversation during which she warned me that I was nearing my expiration date. The only good thing that came from the conversation was that a week later Aunt Daisy Mae showed up on my doorstep with some suitcases and a can of paint. She had been in Borneo up until that point, teaching children to paint, but decided that she wanted a new adventure.

Together with Aunt Daisy Mae and my black Bombay cat Jasper, who was sleeping peacefully in his carrier in the back of the van, I had set off with my (semi) new mobile bookstore, Word Travels. We never looked back. And my brother regularly called me to complain about my mother, who had moved into his spare room. Poor guy.

As we drove through the winding roads leading to Greenwood, I felt unease settling in my stomach.

"Layla hasn't answered any of my texts," I told Aunt Daisy Mae. "She usually confirms before we get there, but she hasn't said anything yet."

"This thing has been set up for like a week, right?" Aunt Daisy Mae asked.

I nodded.

"You worry too much," she said, waving her hand dismissively. "Layla knows we're coming. It's not as if this is our first time doing this. She probably got distracted helping some kid or something at the library. You know how she is."

I did, and that was what worried me. Layla always returned my texts promptly. She was annoyingly punctual and knew how bad my anxiety got if I wasn't sure about something. Layla Johnson was the type of friend who took that sort of thing into consideration. Besides, we had left the campsite before dawn so that we could pick up the books early and get back on the road to our next destination. There was an evening market in a nearby town, and we wanted to get there before the ice cream truck took the best spot.

"I guess," I said, releasing a deep breath.

"See?" Aunt Daisy Mae said, grinning widely. "I'm good for you. You've gotten a lot less nervous ever since we started spending more time together."

I let out an amused chuckle but didn't correct her. Aunt Daisy Mae was the calmest person on earth, which could become a little frustrating when she disregarded things like time, rules, or common boundaries. Somehow, she never got in trouble because people could never stay mad at her. If anything, her lax habits sometimes threatened to drive me over the edge.

My phone started ringing before she could reply, and I quickly answered it.

"Hey, Nomad," a familiar deep voice said.

I felt a small thrill pass through me despite myself. "Noah," I said, my smile widening. Aunt Daisy Mae let out a cooing sound and made a kissing face at me, which I ignored.

"Have you made it to Greenwood yet?" he asked. I could hear him closing a door and guessed that he was leaving his hotel. He was on the road quite a bit, working for a company that insured major fixed assets all over the country. His job was to inspect the assets before setting the premiums, and when the company's clients made a claim, he had to investigate the situation.

"Just a few minutes out of town," I said, shaking my head at Aunt Daisy Mae, who was trying to lean her ear against the back of my phone so that she could hear what he was saying.

"Great, what are your plans for after the night market?"

"I don't know yet," I admitted, giving Aunt Daisy Mae an evil look so that she would sit back in her seat and stop trying to hear our conversation firsthand. "Probably fall asleep after putting everyone back in their cages."

Aunt Daisy Mae pulled a face at me while Noah laughed.

"How about we meet up for a late dinner?" he asked.

"You're going to be in the area?" I asked, my heart beating faster at the prospect of seeing him again.

"Yeah," he said, and I could hear the smile in his voice, "they just let me know. Apparently, there's a new restaurant in town that's been creating a lot of buzz. I thought I could get some food to go if they're any good and meet you at the night market."

"That sounds great," I said, trying not to sound too eager. All the guys I dated back home always said I came on too strong, and I certainly didn't want to scare him away.

"It's a date," he said, and I fought the urge to blush.

"If you don't bag him soon, then I will," Aunt Daisy Mae warned after we said goodbye.

"Please don't." I scrunched my nose at the thought of my aunt flirting with Noah. It would be incredibly uncomfortable.

"I'm just saying," she said, wagging her finger at me, "you don't leave a guy like that on the shelf for too long. He'll be snatched up by another woman in no time!"

"You sound like my mother," I said with a sigh.

"Take that back!" Aunt Daisy Mae gasped, looking offended.

I shook my head at her. At that moment, I spotted Jasper waking up through the rearview mirror. He let out a massive yawn and stretched lazily before sitting in front of the window. Most cats hated being in a vehicle, but Jasper loved it. He spent hours staring at the scenery and had several favorite napping spots in the van.

About half an hour later, we drove into Greenwood. The town was located a few miles away from Burling-ton, Vermont, which gave it a typical small-town feel, but the residents had access to most of the perks that came from living in a city. It was still ten minutes before the library opened. I tried calling Layla to see if she was already at work, but her phone went straight to voicemail. A tide of anxiety rose up inside of me, but I shook my head. There was no way I was going to let it get the best of me again. I couldn't help but feel that something was off, but that was a sensation that I was familiar with.

As we pulled up to the library, I spotted someone running in the opposite direction. It looked like he was terrified and kept looking over his shoulder. I couldn't make out his face, but his actions scared me, so I kept a careful eye out as I pulled into the Greenwood Public Library parking lot.

Layla would never disappoint me. When I started the mobile bookstore business, I had very little money for books. We had kept in touch over the years, and I knew she was very happy as the head librarian in Greenwood. When she'd found out what my plan was, she offered to sell me all the books that were being phased out of the library at a discount. Those books usually went to local secondhand bookstores, and there were plenty of places she could have sold the books to at a higher price, but she was eager to help me achieve my dream. Layla was the kindest person I knew. We had been friends since high school. Us fellow book nerds had to stick together, and she always took that sentiment very seriously.

We waited another twenty minutes before I called Layla again. By then, I knew something was very wrong. Layla was never late. Thankfully, a shiny new car pulled up beside us, and a young woman jumped out. She looked like she was in her early twenties, and her hair had been dyed a pretty shade of lilac.

"Were you guys waiting long?" she asked, looking nervous. "I am so late! Layla is going to kill me."

She dashed off toward the doors of the library before I could say anything.

"Where do you think she got her nose pierced?" Aunt Daisy Mae asked, referring to the girl's septum piercing. "I'd love to get mine done."

"You'd look great, Aunt Daisy Mae," I said with a sigh, knowing that there was no way I could convince her not to get the piercing done.

As we walked up to the library, Jasper jumped out of the car and followed us, his tail swishing slightly as he walked. His fur was so black that he looked like a cat's shadow instead of an actual cat. It made it very easy for him to hide, which frequently led me to believe that he was missing. A part of me thought that he enjoyed giving me a fright.

The Greenwood Public Library was a beautiful building in the middle of the quaint town. The building was at least a hundred years old with stone walls and cozy carpets. It even had a massive fireplace on the one end.

"Hi," the young woman said as soon as we walked into the library, "you must be Claudia Madison? Layla mentioned that you were coming."

"That's me," I said, wondering if I could just head to the Last Chance bookshelf.

After I had bought most of my initial stock from Layla, she'd offered to reserve some Last Chance books for me every few months. They were usually leftover from a semi-annual book sale. The proceeds went to a local charity.

"I'm Melody," she said. "I work with Layla. She isn't in yet, but I'm sure she won't mind if you just get the books."

Melody was a striking young woman. She had fine, delicate features with a shock of lilac hair that fell past her shoulders. Her style was eclectic as she wore a white frilly dress with a gold chain belt and cowboy boots. On anyone else it might have looked strange, but it worked on her.

I wanted to wait for Layla, but we were already running out of time. It was disappointing, but maybe I could swing by in the next few days. We thanked Melody, who began booting up the computer for the day ahead.

As we walked past the bookstacks to the back of the library, the hairs at the back of my neck stood up. I thought I was overreacting, but when I spotted a few books scattered on the ground, Aunt Daisy Mae looked at me with wide eyes. The library was extremely cold, and I felt goosebumps erupt on my arms. We walked a little further, and that's when we noticed the overturned bookcase. There were books everywhere, and someone's shoe had been caught underneath it. Jasper took one look at the scene and bolted, his paws moving soundlessly over the thick carpet.

It took me a few seconds to realize that the shoe was still attached to a foot. I wondered dimly why Layla was lying on the floor, and it didn't occur to me that she was dead until Aunt Daisy Mae screamed in fright.

CHAPTER TWO

*I*t didn't take long for the police to show up. They quickly put tape around the crime scene and made us go into the side room of the library. It was a storage space and the staff room, so there were books everywhere and comfortable couches so that the staff could rest whenever they wanted. Melody was shaking in shock but managed to make us some coffee before the detective arrived.

Detective Roman Sterling was a large man. He was so tall that he had to duck his head slightly when he walked through the door, and he was so wide that it looked like it would take two of Melody to fill his pants. I guessed that he was about fifty years old, since he had gray hair around his temples, but I could have been wrong since he had such a stressful job. For all I knew, he was in his early forties but looked older.

"So," he said, after introducing himself. He sat down on one of the couches with a groan as he surveyed us. "What do we have here?"

We all looked at each other, unsure of who should speak first. None of us had ever been in this situation before.

"Layla is dead, and we found her," Aunt Daisy Mae said simply.

Her words cut through me, and I felt my throat close up. None of it felt real. How could this be happening? I had spoken to Layla the day before, and nothing seemed amiss.

"Yes, that much is apparent," he said, giving her a withering look, and I immediately felt a wave of protectiveness wash over me. I put my arm around Aunt Daisy Mae and glared at him. "Walk me through what happened. Don't leave out any details."

I told him the events of the morning, and he nodded along quietly. When I got to the part about the man running away from the library, he bit his lip slightly.

"So, you're saying that you knew something was wrong when she didn't show up on time for work?" Detective Sterling asked, raising a bushy eyebrow at me. I nodded, and he continued, "Is it possible that you knew something was wrong because you knew she was already dead?"

His words caught me completely off-guard, and I looked at Aunt Daisy Mae in alarm.

"Are you asking if I had anything to do with this?" I asked in shock.

"That's right, sweetheart," he said, sighing impatiently.

"Don't call her sweetheart, you boor," Aunt Daisy Mae snapped.

He ignored her and kept his focus on me. "You got here early; let's say that she wasn't late for work but you intercepted her."

Melody watched the proceedings with wide eyes as she picked at her nails.

"Maybe you two had an argument," Detective Sterling continued, "and things went sideways, so you killed her then split back outside so that people would think you had just arrived. Maybe it was an accident."

"That's impossible," I spat, feeling the room spinning around me. "Layla was my friend. I would never hurt her! What kind of monster would even leave someone like that?"

Detective Sterling's face remained impassive.

"Ask the song girl," Aunt Daisy Mae said, gripping

my hand tightly, "the door was locked when she got here. She had to unlock it."

"Song girl?" Detective Sterling asked in surprise.

"Melody," I said, gesturing at the young woman.

Melody jumped at the sound of her own name and looked at Detective Sterling in fear.

"Well, girl, is it true?" he asked. She nodded quickly and clutched her hands together. I felt sorry for her. No one deserved to be at Detective Sterling's mercy. "How many people have keys to this place?"

"Just me and Layla...sir," Melody said, clearing her throat slightly.

"You're not in the clear yet," Detective Sterling warned me. "Don't leave town until I tell you to. We might have more questions."

"What?" Aunt Daisy Mae protested. "You can't do that! We have to be at—"

"What time did you leave last night?" Detective Sterling asked Melody, interrupting Aunt Daisy Mae, which caused her to turn red and sputter in anger.

"Afternoon," Melody answered quickly. "I had a gig in the city, and Layla let me go early. She knew I had to rehearse and everything."

Detective Sterling grunted and tapped his leg thoughtfully.

"Is that it?" Aunt Daisy Mae asked angrily. "You put my niece through the wringer then let her off so easy?"

"Aunt Daisy Mae," I said softly, giving Melody an apologetic glance, "there's no need to rake her over the coals, too. She doesn't have anything to do with this. She's just as distraught as us."

Melody gave me a grateful smile then looked at Detective Sterling warily.

"Don't tell me how to do my job," Detective Sterling told Aunt Daisy Mae. His phone began ringing loudly, preventing my aunt from launching into an angry tirade. I wondered where Jasper was and hoped that he was staying safe. He was capable of keeping himself hidden until things were calm, but who knew what would happen if Detective Sterling caught him.

"Go for Sterling," he said, raising his voice as he likely sensed that Aunt Daisy Mae was on the verge of yelling at him. He listened attentively to the person on the other end, a deep frown forming on his face.

I took a moment to take a deep breath and try to settle my anxiety. My hands were shaking, and I felt ice-cold. The shock would start wearing off soon, and I knew I'd need to lie down or get something to eat.

"Detain him," Detective Sterling barked, causing me to jump in fright. He got to his feet and swept out of the room, leaving us to stare after him incredulously.

We sat in uncomfortable silence for a few minutes before Aunt Daisy Mae scoffed loudly.

"I'm just going to come out and say it," she said, raising her hands as if in surrender, "I don't like that man. Someone needs to deck him."

"Aunt Daisy Mae," I chided, even though I secretly agreed with her, "you know violence is never the answer."

"I don't know that," Aunt Daisy Mae said as she got up and left the room. I heard her calling for Jasper and shook my head at her. She was going to get us in trouble one day.

I had almost forgotten that Melody was in the room, and when she shuffled her feet, it startled me. She grimaced apologetically.

"Do you think we're suspects now?" Melody asked me, her eyes wide with fear.

I mulled her words over. It certainly appeared that way, but it didn't feel real. How could anyone think that we had anything to do with Layla's death? The mere fact that she was dead hadn't sunk in yet, and my head felt like it was trapped in a vice.

"I'm not sure," I decided, "but we should be careful not to do anything to get on his radar."

Melody nodded somberly. "I'm sorry your visit had to end this way," she said absently.

At that moment, Aunt Daisy Mae walked into the room holding Jasper in her arms. He had a bewildered expression on his face, and when a policeman walked past him, he hissed angrily. Usually, he hated it when people held him, but at that moment, he was clinging to Aunt Daisy Mae's voluminous shirt as if his life depended on it.

"Come on, girly," Aunt Daisy Mae said, glaring at the policeman that Jasper had hissed at. The poor man hadn't done anything wrong and looked extremely uncomfortable with the hostility that he was receiving. "It's time to go. We need to set up, since we're going to be here awhile."

That night, I was sitting outside our tent at the camping grounds, watching the stars. Our van was parked only a few feet from the tent. Inside, the van looked like a miniature library. With all the seats removed from the back, I had installed shelves to hold the three thousand books we transported and sold. Each bookshelf had a little wooden bar in the front which kept the books from falling out when we were on the road. The vehicle was equipped with small kitchen appliances, a tiny workspace, and some storage space beneath the floor.

Everything we owned could fit into our van and the little trailer we towed behind us. When we unloaded our gear from the trailer, it only took a short time to set up the tent and our camping beds. It was a simple way of life, but we'd never been happier.

Headlights caught my attention, and I saw a car making its way toward us. Noah. My heart stopped, and I felt a wave of guilt overwhelm me.

"I'm so sorry!" I said as soon as he stepped out of the car. "My phone is on silent... It's been such a long day; you'll never believe what happened."

"Hey," Noah said, shaking his head slightly. "I heard. They announced her death on the radio earlier, and when I couldn't get hold of you, I figured that you were probably massively overwhelmed."

My eyes filled with tears, and I quickly turned away. I spotted the tent flap rustling and guessed that Aunt Daisy Mae must have told him where to find us. She was a gem of a woman. Noah sat down next to me and listened intently as I told him about what had happened. In the meantime, Jasper wandered out of the tent, and when he spotted Noah, he ran up to him and wound himself in between his legs.

"Sounds intense," Noah said when I finally finished my story. "What are you going to do, Clauds?"

"I don't know," I admitted, resting my face in my

hands. "I miss her so much; I can't believe that she's gone, and now someone thinks that I might have done this to her. It's…insane."

Noah grimaced and took my hand in his. It felt nice.

"I don't think you should roll over and let them think you had anything to do with this," Noah said firmly. "You knew her very well; this Sterling guy doesn't know anything about her. Maybe you could help him find out the truth."

I sat up straight. The thought hadn't occurred to me, but it made sense. Maybe I could help, and I could prove Sterling wrong. Noah's chocolate-brown eyes warmed at my expression, and he smiled, revealing a slight dimple in his right cheek. He was taller than me, even when we were sitting down, so I had to look up at him when we were talking, and his long legs stretched out ahead of him.

"You know what?" I said thoughtfully. "You make an excellent point. Layla wouldn't have wanted me to hide away from this. I'm going to do everything I can to find out who did this to her. It's the least I can do."

CHAPTER THREE

oah left sometime after our talk, and I couldn't believe the effect he had on my mood. It was as if he had shone a whole new light on my situation. I wasn't helpless; I could actually do something. Even if it didn't make a difference, then at least I wasn't sitting around feeling sorry for myself, and that made all the difference. After he left, I went to bed and that's when all the emotions of the day hit me. I cried myself to sleep as I realized that I would never be able to share book ideas with Layla or talk about the books we both were reading. She was a special kind of friend in that we almost seemed to share a mind, and I'd miss that. It was hard to find a friend who had the same intellectual mindset.

Aunt Daisy Mae made me hot chocolate while I cried, and Jasper tried to help by lying close to my side. It was touching, but it also made it hard to move. Even though he pinned me down, I would never move him, in case he got offended and left.

The next morning, I woke up with puffy eyes and a heavy heart. The sun hadn't risen yet, so I just lay there staring at the top part of the tent. Aunt Daisy Mae snored merrily in her bed, and when it was light enough, I slipped out of bed quietly in order not to wake her up.

I decided to go for a run and headed toward town. The scenery was beautiful, and I breathed in the fresh air as I ran. It wasn't long before I came across a little coffee shop. It was just around the corner from the library, and the thought of running past the library filled my stomach with dread, so I headed into the coffee shop so that I wouldn't have to see the library.

The shop was quite full, and I guessed that it was a popular breakfast spot. I decided to get in line for some coffee—it would take something strong to get Aunt Daisy Mae out of bed. The two women in front of me had strollers with them and were wearing exercise clothing similar to mine.

"I just can't believe Layla's dead," the first mom said,

pushing her stroller back and forth, likely hoping that the motion would keep her baby asleep. "She was such a doll."

A heavy lump developed in my throat.

"I liked her, but I guess this just goes to show that nothing is ever as it seems," the second mother said, shaking her head sadly. "I mean, she must have made someone super angry for them to resort to murder!"

My hands clenched into fists, and I bit back an angry retort. Why were they blaming the victim?

"Do you think it was an angry ex-lover?" The first mother gasped, her face alight with anticipation. "She was really pretty, you know, when she did her makeup and stuff."

"Maybe," the second mother said, inspecting her nails lazily, "but my money is on Kara. She's really lost it lately. Did you know that she petitioned the mayor to install security cameras in the town square to scare off potential loiterers?"

The first mother scoffed and rolled her eyes, but my ears prickled.

"She always had a problem with Layla," the second mother continued with smug self-assurance. "I heard someone saw them fighting the day that Layla died."

"Seriously?" the first mother asked.

I hoped they would say more, but at that moment, they reached the front counter and got distracted with their coffee orders. By the time I had my coffee, they were already gone, and I wanted to kick myself for not running after them. When I got back to the campsite, I used the coffee to lure Aunt Daisy Mae out of bed. She immediately set up her art supplies and began painting, and I found myself with the rare luxury of having nothing to do. It was infuriating.

Instead of sitting down with a good book, I decided to start my project. Noah probably hadn't meant that I should investigate the case, but the idea had come to me while I listened to the gossiping mothers. With that goal in mind, I began setting up a "murder board." I pinned a picture of Layla in the middle of the board with a list of everything I knew about that day, which wasn't much. Then I made a note of what I had heard at the coffee shop. I was so absorbed in my task that I didn't hear Melody's car drive up to the campsite.

"Hey!" Melody called out as she got out of the car.

Aunt Daisy Mae was preoccupied with her painting and didn't even acknowledge Melody. When I got out of the van, I found Melody staring at Aunt Daisy Mae with a bewildered expression.

"Oh yeah, you're not going to get anything out of

her," I said apologetically. "When she's painting, she's transported to another world, and there's nothing anyone can do about it."

"Okay," Melody said, drawing out the word and looking at Aunt Daisy Mae with a skeptical expression. "Uh, so I just came over with those books that Layla promised you. I figured that you could keep yourself busy until Detective Sterling gets back to us."

A small smile stretched over my face. "Wow, how thoughtful. I can see why Layla hired you."

Melody blushed and looked away. A flash of pain crossed her face, and I felt guilty for bringing Layla up when the wound was obviously still raw.

I helped her get the books out of her car, and as we worked, I found myself looking over at her. Finally, I worked up the nerve to ask the question that was bugging me.

"Do you know someone called Kara?" I asked quickly, as if it wasn't a strange question.

"Kara?" Melody echoed. "Do you mean Kara Meyer?"

"I think so," I said, and gave her a brief explanation of where I had heard the name.

"Of course," Melody said, slapping her forehead lightly, "how did I not think of Kara? She was always fighting with Layla. She has some…strong opinions, and

"What is this about?" she asked. "Why are you asking me that?"

"Give it a rest, Kara," Melody said, rolling her eyes exasperatedly. "People saw you two fighting. It's better you tell us so that we can tell the police that it was no big deal."

"You're right," I said, looking at Melody gratefully. "The police are going to find out about this, and we need to make sure that we have our stories straight before we talk to them. We wouldn't want to implicate you unnecessarily. We just want to make sure that the police don't waste any time on people who obviously aren't guilty."

Kara relaxed as I rambled, and her forehead wrinkles disappeared as she stopped frowning.

"That's kind of you," Kara said, shifting her weight slightly. "Yeah, we had an argument on the day that she died, but I had no idea that was going to happen. I just wanted her to change her mind about the banned book list."

"Layla refused to ban any books unless they promoted hate speech," Melody told me helpfully.

"That's not quite true." Kara sniffed. "She was quite all right with exposing our youth to radical ideas and inflammatory subject matter."

Melody rolled her eyes but didn't say anything.

"I'm guessing that she refused to revise her list," I

said, my mouth twitching in amusement. Layla hated banning books unless they deserved it. She strongly opposed censorship and claimed that it was the ultimate tool of would-be oppressors.

"She told me to go to..." Kara raised her voice then quickly dropped her volume and looked around cautiously. "H-E-double-hockey-sticks! Can you imagine that? That library has become a heathen den."

"For the last time, the *Hunger Games* books aren't going to turn our children into terrorists," Melody said in annoyance.

"They are violent and immoral, and I stand by my beliefs," Kara said, turning up her nose at Melody. "Layla was determined to impose her radical beliefs on our children, and someone had to stop her. I guess I wasn't the only person who felt that way."

Her words were like an explosion in my ears, and I stood there, looking at her in shock. Melody also froze, an unreadable expression dropping over her face.

"I'm sorry to be so blunt, but there you have it," Kara continued with a shrug. "She was much too opinionated and strong-willed. It looks like that finally caught up to her. Don't get me wrong, it's tragic, but I'm just saying that if she had kept her mouth shut and known her place, then perhaps she would still be alive."

I clenched my fists, but Melody went a step further.

Her nostrils flared, and she glared at Kara with intense hatred.

"I'm not surprised that she got what was coming to her," Kara said.

I managed to pull Melody back just in time to keep her from slapping Kara.

CHAPTER FOUR

"*I* know hitting people is wrong!" Melody covered her face with her hands as we sat in the car. "I know it! I just couldn't stop myself. What is wrong with her? Why would she say such awful, horrible things about Layla?"

I rubbed her back soothingly. While I didn't condone Melody's actions, I could understand where she was coming from. I had to stop myself from screaming at Kara when she had said all those things, and it was so easy to lose control during such an emotional time.

"Layla would have been so disappointed in me," Melody said, shaking her head slowly. "She gave me a chance to be better and I just...I gave in so easily! Do you think Kara will really be able to get me arrested?"

"No, no. And if she goes to the police with this, they're going to start asking questions about why we were there. If she tells them what she told us, then she'll become their number one suspect. I think she was just trying to scare you. Besides, I stopped you before you could actually assault her, so there's no harm done."

After I stopped Melody from hitting Kara, we had left as quickly as possible. Kara had started screaming as if she had been hit and threatened to call the police on us.

"You know I was nothing before Layla gave me this job?" Melody said. "My father threw me out of the house after graduation because I didn't want to go to college. I would have been homeless if she hadn't helped. It's been a few years now, and I don't know where I would have ended up if it wasn't for her. What do I do now? Where do I go? Layla was like my family, and now she's gone."

"Hey," I said gently, putting my arm around her shoulders. It meant that I had to twist myself uncomfortably over the car's center console, but it was worth it. "Layla was so proud of you. She always mentioned her stellar assistant. Look, this is a horrible tragedy. I don't know how we're going to get through it but we will. We have to keep the library going. Layla would have appreciated that."

Melody nodded slowly and looked up at me.

"Layla believed in your dreams," I said, pulling back to give her space. "So you keep doing what you've been doing. Work at the library until your dreams come true. Then you can dedicate your first album to Layla."

"I can't name a song after her because that's already been done." Melody gave a wry smile.

"She really hated that song," I said, shaking my head as I remembered how she used to rant about how unfortunate it was that her name was in a song. Whenever someone sang her name, she pursed her lips and glared at them until the song withered on their lips.

Melody's smile grew, and I felt my spirits lift a little. My grief still sat in my heart like a rock, but it eased a little when I was able to help someone else. We sat in the car for a little while longer until Melody asked me to help her sort out some books at the library. I wanted to say no, but I knew that if I didn't push through my discomfort at seeing the library, it would only grow until I could never go into the building that Layla loved so much.

My only condition was that we picked up Aunt Daisy Mae and Jasper first. Aunt Daisy Mae wasn't done with her painting yet, so she brought all her supplies with her and set up outside the library. Jasper was happy to be back at the library and spent his time exploring the shelves.

When I walked up to the overturned bookcase where they had found Layla, I could feel the blood rushing through my ears. The image of her body under the bookcase would forever be seared into the back of my eyelids.

"The police finished clearing up the scene yesterday," Melody explained, gulping slightly as she looked at the bookcase.

It was comforting to know that I wasn't the only one who was so affected by the sight of the bookcase. It hurt to look at it, but it didn't just hurt me which meant that I wasn't overreacting.

"And they left this for us," I said grimly. "How considerate of them."

We began picking up the books, and I fought the urge to burn every book on the shelf. It was the geography section, and I doubted that anyone would miss a book explaining the various types of geodes. However, Layla always said that only bigots burned books, and she would have been very angry if I burned any books. On the other hand, maybe she would have understood the urge. What would Layla have done if I was the one who had been murdered?

There was no doubt in my mind that she wouldn't have rested until she knew what had happened to me. It was strange; Layla was gone but I couldn't stop myself from imagining what she would be doing if she was still alive. It was comforting, as if a part of her was still there with me.

Melody and I worked together to lift the bookcase. When it was up and we began packing the books back, I couldn't help but shiver at the eeriness of our task. It looked like nothing had happened, and that seemed very wrong.

Thankfully, a loud crash distracted me from my task. I shared a bewildered look with Melody, but then I spotted Jasper running past us at high speed.

"I better go check what he wrecked," I said with a sigh, which caused Melody to smile slightly.

Jasper cautiously followed me, and when I found a pile of books on the floor a few feet from where we had been working, I put my hands on my hips and gave him a stern look.

"Naughty boy," I scolded, "we're busy working hard to put all the books back, and you're just knocking them off."

Jasper made a chirruping sound and immediately rolled on his back, exposing his fluffy belly. I tried to maintain my stern expression, but it was impossible. I kneeled down and scratched his tummy before turning to pick up the books. Jasper wasn't happy about that and got up. He followed my hand and nipped me as I reached for a book.

"Stop being a brat," I chided, and he sat down while giving me an innocent look.

I sighed loudly and sat on the floor. He immediately turned on his back again, and I began massaging his tummy and cooing over him. Jasper always became testy when I didn't give him the attention that he felt he deserved. He began purring loudly and wound his paw around my hand, indicating his contentment.

My position on the floor gave me a perfect vantage point of the bottom of the bookcase, and I began looking through the titles on the bottom shelf as Jasper purred. Something caught my eye, and I let go of Jasper to reach under the shelf. He meowed in protest and immediately sauntered off with an indignant air.

I usually wouldn't have stopped petting him until he got up on his own, but this was infinitely more important. Layla's phone. I couldn't believe that the cops hadn't spotted it while they were gathering evidence. It only solidified my belief that I was doing the right thing by conducting my own investigation.

Melody hummed to herself while she worked, and I sensed that she wasn't paying any attention to me. I switched on the phone and was blown away by the sheer number of notifications on Layla's phone. She almost never answered her messages and mostly forgot about her phone.

I went to her call log and spotted my own number at the top. Below that was a number of calls from a blocked number. The last call was on the day that Layla died. It looked like the person had stopped calling right before she died. A shiver ran down my spine. Someone had been trying to reach her desperately all day but had stopped right before she died. That couldn't have been a coincidence. I quickly went to her texts and found a thread containing the blocked number.

Layla, answer me.

I'm serious.

Stop being so childish.

I just want to talk.

Layla.

Whatever. You're not that special.

Any woman would be lucky to have me.

Who do you think you are?????

ANSWER YOUR PHONE!!!!!!!!!!!!

Layla

Layla

Layla

You're a hateful desperate loser

No one will ever love you

You're going to regret this so much

Okay, I'm sorry. Please just text me.

I just want to know that you're okay.

The texts became increasingly desperate, swinging from desperate to threatening to apologetic. I felt sick reading them and wanted to cry. Poor Layla. The sheer number of calls and texts amounted to harassment, and I wondered why she hadn't told me about anything. She only answered once.

Jason, stop.

Jason obviously ignored her request because there were a barrage of texts and calls after she had replied. The last one caused me to go cold with fear.

I'm coming over.

The time stamp indicated that it was sent a few minutes before his last call. I sat there for a few moments and wondered what I should do with the information. It was obvious that Layla didn't want anything to do with Jason, and that he was somewhat unhinged. This phone needed to make it to the police, but I wondered if they would do anything with the information, especially since they hadn't managed to find her phone at all.

It occurred to me that Melody had stopped humming, and I quickly shoved the phone in my pocket as she walked past.

"Melody, do you know anyone named Jason?"

She stopped short and looked at me in surprise.

"I don't know where you keep getting your information," Melody said with a laugh, "but this is scary. How do you know about Jason?"

I shrugged lightly and bit my lip. I wasn't sure if I wanted to tell Melody about the phone. She would probably insist that we go to the police. Besides, if the police found out about what I was doing then I really didn't want her to be implicated in any way.

It had occurred to me that I could get into a lot of trouble. The old me would have been shocked and would never have even considered taking part in an investigation like that. However, I had changed a lot over the years, and I felt that this was what needed to be done. It was Layla. She was one of the best friends I had ever had, and if it wasn't for her then I likely wouldn't have been able to start my mobile bookshop in the first place. Layla had shown me how to be brave, and now it was time to show what I had learned from her.

"Okay," Melody said, drawing out the word slowly, "Layla and Jason dated a few months ago. You know how private she was about her love life. She didn't tell me much. I'm surprised that she didn't tell you anything."

"Maybe she was waiting to see what happened first," I said, nodding slowly. Layla never told me about her boyfriends unless it was a serious relationship. She wasn't the type to make a fuss about a new relationship and didn't get attached easily. It appeared as though Jason didn't have the same views on relationships.

"Maybe," Melody said simply. "Why don't you go talk to him? He works just around the corner. He's a lawyer."

CHAPTER FIVE

asper was still annoyed with me, which meant that I had to bribe him with his favorite fish snacks before he would finally leave the library. I decided not to take Melody with me to Jason's office. While she had been very helpful, I wasn't willing to tell her about Layla's cellphone yet. Thankfully, Aunt Daisy Mae was taking a break from her painting, so she was willing to accompany me.

"When the muse takes a break, so must I," Aunt Daisy Mae explained as she cleaned her hands with an old rag. "It would be useless to continue without her."

I nodded sagely, as if I completely understood what she was talking about. Aunt Daisy Mae often gave me lectures about the importance of her muse. While I respected her artistic talent, I had to admit that her

muse tended to make appearances at the most convenient times. For example, the muse often chose to call
when it was time to unpack or pack the van. It was like
clockwork; once there was a lot of work to be done, the
muse would arrive, and Aunt Daisy Mae would be
powerless to resist her.

"Of course," I said patiently.

It wasn't hard to find Jason's law firm. It was the only
one in town and was located in an old townhouse that
had been converted into an office.

"I hate it when businesses do this to lovely old houses," Aunt Daisy Mae said with a mournful sigh. "Why
don't they just stick to their horrid modern buildings
and leave these homes alone?"

"It's a travesty," I said absently, trying to think of
what I was going to say to Jason. This investigation
involved a lot more people skills than I had at my
disposal.

"Why aren't you more upset by this?" Aunt Daisy
Mae asked, gesturing at the sign that had been drilled
into the old sandstone. "Usually, you'd be the one to rant
about this sort of thing."

Glancing at the sign that read, "Diggs Law Offices,
Inc," I gave Aunt Daisy Mae a tight smile but walked into
the building before I had to respond. She followed me

with a huff, and I could feel her suspicious gaze boring a hole into my back.

"We're here to see Jason," I told the receptionist. "We're friends of Layla's."

The receptionist, a young woman in her early twenties, gave me a bored once-over before continuing to type on her phone. It took her about five minutes to finish her text before she finally went into Jason's office.

I bit my lip nervously.

"I'm guessing that we aren't invited guests," Aunt Daisy Mae said.

"Not quite," I said, picking at my nails.

She slapped my hand and gave me a stern look. I immediately stopped picking at my nails, but the urge to fidget with something made my fingers itch.

The receptionist appeared and ignored us. I had no option but to wait and see what happened. We didn't wait long before Jason walked out of the office. He was a tall, striking man with piercing blue eyes and jet-black hair. His face was tanned, and he had the physique of someone who worked out often. His looks surprised me because Layla had always been more drawn to the quiet, bookish type. It saddened me to think that the change in her taste of men may have had fatal consequences.

"Ladies," he said with a broad smile, showing off

perfectly straight, white teeth, "please, join me in my office for some refreshments."

Aunt Daisy Mae looked over at me and wiggled her eyebrows suggestively. I felt sick. If I had shown her the texts that he had sent to Layla, she probably would have kicked him the moment she saw him. Which was precisely why I had decided to withhold that particular information.

"You said you were friends of Layla's?" Jason asked as we walked into his office. "Such a shame what happened to her. You never think this sort of thing will happen in a town like Greenwood."

Jason's office was a large, spacious room with a massive ornate desk in the middle, leather armchairs, and bookshelves that took up the entire back wall. Suddenly it made sense why Layla had agreed to go out with him.

"It really was," Aunt Daisy Mae said, giving him her most charming smile. "She was such a sweetie. We're going to miss her. Especially Claudia over here."

I nodded. It wasn't hard to look devastated. I couldn't bring myself to look at Jason. Every time I looked at him, I imagined him creeping through the bookstacks, stalking Layla. I saw him push her violently into the bookshelves while she screamed. I felt him look

at me curiously and hoped that he mistook my reluc-
tance to look at him as me being shy.

"I see," Jason said thoughtfully.

"How did you know our beloved Layla?" Aunt Daisy
Mae asked, sitting down in one of the armchairs.

"We were dating," Jason said with a mournful sigh.

"Oh?" Aunt Daisy Mae said. She gave me a sharp
look, and I shrugged before sitting next to her.

"Didn't Layla tell you about me?" A slight frown
developed between Jason's eyebrows.

"She did," I lied quickly. "That's why I thought I had
to check on you while I'm in town."

"Layla would have appreciated that," he said with a
smile. "I'm afraid that we weren't very serious though. I
would have liked to get to know her more, but Layla was
always so private. It was hard to get through to her. And
I'm a busy man, so I probably didn't give her the attention she required."

I nodded slowly, as though I completely agreed with
him, even though I knew that every word that came out
of his mouth was probably a lie.

"How were things going with you two?" I asked. "I
hadn't spoken to Layla in a while. We were supposed to
catch up while I was in town."

Jason sighed as he sat down behind his massive desk.

He put his arms on the fancy leather armrests of his chair and leaned back with a troubled expression.

"Layla was…" he trailed off, as if trying to find the right words to describe her, "a sweet girl. She had all these strange ideas, but I think we could have made a long-term relationship work. I decided that we needed to take a break for a while. Just so that she could get her priorities straight, you know?"

I couldn't force myself to nod. He was a pig.

"Everyone in town warned me that she was an odd duck," he continued, "but I decided to take a chance with her. It went well, but then she became all moody. I don't know what was wrong with her, but I tried my best to help her. One day, she just decided to take a short break. I've been trying to win her back."

Aunt Daisy Mae smiled sweetly at him, and I felt like throwing up.

"Did you care about her?" I asked.

"Yes," Jason said, looking appropriately mournful, "she had a lot of potential. Like I said, we could have had a strong relationship, which was why I was trying to win her back. She was being impossible, but I knew that it was only a matter of time before we patched things up again."

"Did you see her that day?" I asked, ignoring his sugary words.

He frowned at me and shook his head slowly. "You know, Detective Sterling already asked me all of this. If you'd like, you can go speak to him."

This surprised me, and I looked at him. He was smiling slightly at me, as if he'd been waiting for me to turn to him. Layla had been smart to break up with him.

"I'm sorry," I said with a sheepish grin, "I'm just so shocked by all of this. I want to know as much about that last day as possible."

Jason nodded, his expression full of pity. "No, I'm sorry, I didn't see her that day. She needed some space, and I was happy to give it to her. I was willing to do whatever she needed. Like I said, she was such a sweet woman."

I nodded gratefully, but inside I was seething. We left shortly afterward, and I fought the urge to go back inside and tell him that I knew all about his texts.

"What a disgusting man," Aunt Daisy Mae said thoughtfully.

"What?" I asked in surprise. "You looked like you were going to ask him out at any second."

"He's handsome, to be sure," Aunt Daisy Mae said dismissively, "which means he's probably got an ego the size of Texas. Men like that expect everyone to find them handsome. I was simply obliging so that he'd give us what we wanted."

I looked at her in awe, and she winked at me.

"Why don't we ask Melody what really happened between those two?" Aunt Daisy Mae suggested. "A man rarely tells the truth when a woman rejects him. His mild condescension was a bright red warning flag."

As we made our way back to the library, I explained what I had found. Jasper was in the back of the van, playing with a paper bag that I had put there to keep him busy while we spoke to Jason. Usually, Jasper tired himself out with a paper bag then fell asleep. By the time we made it to the library, the bag was in shreds, and he was sleeping innocently on a blanket I left for him on the shelf.

Melody was still working in the library when we got there. Her cheeks were slightly wet, and her eyes were red, which meant that she had probably been crying while we were gone. My heart clenched painfully when I saw her face, and I gave her a comforting smile.

"How did it go?" Melody asked. "Did Jason agree to speak to you?"

"Oh yes," Aunt Daisy Mae said with a smile. "He said that Layla had asked for some time apart, and he was happy to oblige. It seems like he really respected her opinion."

Melody snorted derisively and shook her head.

Aunt Daisy Mae shot me a knowing look, and I

couldn't help but be impressed by her intuition. She understood human nature better than anyone I knew. It was a very useful gift as it made her a natural salesperson. She sold more books than I could ever sell. Once she got someone to spend over a thousand dollars on old books in one go.

"Was that not the case?" Aunt Daisy Mae asked curiously.

"No," Melody said firmly, "that guy was obsessed with her. She was so stressed when they were dating. If she did anything wrong, he would fight with her or give her the silent treatment. Finally, she broke things off and told him to leave her alone. She even blocked his number, but he just got a new one so that he could contact her."

"I'm guessing that he didn't leave her alone then," I said, feeling Layla's phone burn a hole through my pocket.

"He got worse." Melody shook her head in disgust. "He kept showing up and begging her to take him back. We'd find flowers at the door every morning. It was ridiculous. Our trash began looking like a nursery. No matter what she did, he wouldn't stop. Then he'd stop by and ask if she got his flowers."

"He sent those every day?" Aunt Daisy Mae asked, looking disgusted.

I shook my head. Poor Layla must have been so frustrated. There was nothing worse than a man who couldn't accept the word "no."

"Well," Melody said with a frown, "every day for months except on the morning when we found her body."

CHAPTER SIX

$\mathcal{I}$ was busy reviewing the information I had collected that day when I heard another van pull up to the camping spot next to ours. I assumed that it was just another camper, but when Jasper got up and ran toward the sound, I knew that it could only be one person.

When I went outside, my suspicions were confirmed.

"Hey, Claudia," Ellie said, holding Jasper in her arms. He was lying on his back and purring profusely as she rubbed the back of his head.

"Ellie," I said, giving her a tight hug, causing Jasper to meow at me indignantly, "thank you so much for coming."

Ellie McBrine owned a mobile coffee shop, which meant that we saw each other frequently. While Layla had been the one to give me books for the mobile book-shop, Ellie was the one who encouraged me to start the business in the first place. She was a tall, willowy woman with dark brown hair and thick glasses.

"I couldn't leave you like this," Ellie said. "I was shocked when I heard about Layla... I'm so sorry. She really didn't deserve to die like that. Do the police know what happened yet?"

"Those policemen wouldn't know how to find their way out of a plastic bag let alone how to find a murder-er," Aunt Daisy Mae said, walking out of the tent with a flourish. She always loved to make an entrance.

"I'm sure that's not true," Ellie said, turning to me with an alarmed expression.

I grimaced and nodded. She shook her head in disbe-lief. We helped her settle in for the night, and as we worked, I told her about the events of the past few days.

"I can't believe Detective Sterling would treat you that way," Ellie said incredulously. "Can't you report him or something?"

"What?" Aunt Daisy Mae scoffed. "Then we run the risk of looking even guiltier to him. He's a little man with too much power."

I looked at her quizzically and demonstrated how tall the detective was. Aunt Daisy Mae gave me a with-ering look while Ellie chuckled.

"You know what I mean," Aunt Daisy Mae said, rolling her eyes in annoyance. "Anyway, if we complain then he will undoubtedly retaliate. It would be better if we stayed off his radar until we have conclusive proof that we're innocent."

"I disagree," Ellie said simply.

I looked at her in surprise while Aunt Daisy Mae pursed her lips in distaste. This wasn't new. Ellie often disagreed with Aunt Daisy Mae. Sometimes I thought of Aunt Daisy Mae as the devil on my shoulder while Ellie was the angel. I could always count on her to advise me to do the right thing. She had a firm sense of right and wrong. Ellie followed the law down to the letter and always advised others to do the same.

Her father had been a gambler and a conman who moved his family all over the country. She had seen firsthand what happened when someone chose to ignore the difference between right and wrong.

"What would you suggest?" I asked.

"You've got plenty of information," Ellie pointed out. "If you hold onto that phone, you're obstructing justice. The police have the resources to do this properly. What if they can find stuff that you can't but you're not giving them the chance to do their jobs because you're holding onto vital information. They're probably searching high and low for that phone. What if they don't find enough evidence and the murderer walks free?"

Her words struck fear into my heart. I hadn't even considered what would happen if I failed. What if my actions meant that the entire case fell apart when it went to trial? It was such a scary feeling. I looked over at the van where I had put the phone.

"You're right," I said as Aunt Daisy Mae groaned. "I'll head over to the station tomorrow and tell them absolutely everything. Thank you."

Ellie nodded and gave me a comforting hug. We spent the rest of the evening chatting and catching up. Aunt Daisy Mae went to bed early, and I knew that she was upset about my decision, but Ellie made a lot of sense. If I hindered justice in any way, I knew I would regret it for the rest of my life.

The next morning, Ellie left early but promised to return for the funeral. She took some of our books to sell on the road since we were still stuck in one spot. While I was sad to see her go, I understood that she needed to get back to selling coffee. She was supporting her younger brother who was attending New York University.

"I don't think we should do this," Aunt Daisy Mae said as we parked outside the police station. "You know I love Ellie, but she wasn't here for everything. She never even met Detective Sterling. I'd bet that if she knew the type of person he was, then she wouldn't have suggested that we do this."

"Come on, Aunt Daisy Mae," I said brightly, even though I felt scared inside, "we need to do this. You know you'd hate for the murderer to go free."

She grumbled but got out of the van while I put Jasper in his cat carrier. It was a simple backpack with a cushion at the bottom and a clear plastic window with airholes for him to look through. He didn't mind being in the carrier for about an hour or so, but when he got impatient, I had to take him out before he began howling.

The police station was a simple brick building on the outskirts of town. It was quiet inside as everyone worked at their cubicles. I spotted a sign that pointed out the direction of the holding cells and looked away uncomfortably. The receptionist led us to Detective Sterling's office.

"This looks nice, cozy," Aunt Daisy Mae said as the receptionist led us into the room.

Unlike Jason's office, Sterling's office was slightly larger than a broom closet with a cheap desk that was piled high with paperwork. We sat in uncomfortable plastic chairs as we waited for him to arrive. When he finally walked in, it was clear to see that he was in no mood to deal with us.

"Hello, ladies," he said with a tense smile, "what can I do for you today?"

I could tell that he was working hard to be polite, so I quickly explained why we had come. When I mentioned Kara, his eyebrows drew together, and I could tell that he was confused. Worse still, he didn't seem to know who Jason was either. Obviously, Jason had lied about talking to the detective. Finally, when I put the phone on the desk, he looked at me with a thoughtful expression.

"So, you're telling me that you just magically happened to find this under a bookcase?" he asked skeptically.

My cheeks turned bright red, and Aunt Daisy Mae gave me a knowing look.

"No, I found it a few feet away from where we found Layla," I said, feeling anger rise within me. "Your boys should have found it, not me."

"You're right," Sterling said, regarding me carefully. "It's strange that they didn't find it. How could they possibly have missed something like that? Unless…"

"Don't start with that nonsense," I said, losing my temper and glaring at him. "Don't pin this on me. Your team was incompetent. Have your techs search through that thing; there's no reason why I would hide that from you. In fact, I'm begging you to search through it. Maybe you'll finally find a suspect."

Sterling leaned back in his chair while Aunt Daisy Mae gave me an enthusiastic thumbs up. Jasper was sitting in the carrier on my lap, and I heard him hiss angrily at Sterling.

Finally, after what felt like an eternity, Sterling shrugged. "Thank you for bringing this to us. However, we already have someone in custody."

"What?" I asked, feeling floored.

"Yes," Sterling said, the corners of his mouth twitching into what I assumed would be a smug smirk. "According to locals, a vagrant by the name of Steve frequented the library. You even saw him that day. He was the one who was running away from the library. We caught him trying to leave town on the day we found the body."

The way he said "the body" made me want to scream and throw things at him. Layla wasn't just a body. She had been a dear friend, and I missed her so much it hurt.

"Why would Steve want to kill Layla?" Aunt Daisy Mae asked incredulously.

"I'm afraid that's privileged information." Sterling let out a long sigh. "You see, that's what police do. While you've been chasing after rumors, we've been getting our job done. Go home, leave this alone now. There's nothing you can do. Just don't leave town yet; we might have some more questions for you."

I nodded absently as I got up to leave. I felt as though the floor had been ripped out from under me. Something didn't feel right. I had seen Steve run away from the library, but I found myself doubting Sterling's words.

After Aunt Daisy Mae closed the door behind us, she put a hand on my shoulder and led me toward some blue plastic chairs.

"I don't like this," she said in a low tone. "We can't give up now, girly. We need to get to the bottom of this."

"I know," I said, looking around, "I'm going to sneak back to the holding cells and talk to him. Can you keep an eye out and warn me if anyone goes in that direction?"

Aunt Daisy Mae regarded me carefully then smiled wickedly. She took the cat carrier out of my hands and opened the zipper. Jasper watched her with intense interest, and once the flap was open, he jumped out of the carrier. A policeman walked past, and Jasper immediately hissed. He slapped the man's leg with his paw and jumped onto a nearby desk. The policeman protested loudly and tried to catch Jasper, but the cat was too quick for him. Soon, about three policemen and the receptionist were doing their best to catch the sly cat.

I was impressed by how quickly Jasper turned everything into chaos. He seemed pleased by his efforts, and I could tell that he was having the time of his life. I trusted that Aunt Daisy Mae would keep him safe. While everyone was trying to get the cat under control, I quickly slipped into the holding cell area.

It was a windowless room divided into cells. There was no privacy, and the harsh fluorescent lights reflected off the steel toilets. I shivered in disgust and looked around for Steve. Thankfully, most of the cells were empty, and I was spared from having to deal with other conflicts. The two cells right at the end of the room were occupied. The first held a sleeping woman who looked like she'd been in a fight, while the second held a big, hulking man who looked almost as large as a professional football player. His hair was grimy, and his clothes had certainly seen better days.

The commotion outside told me that I was still safe, but I felt horribly exposed standing in between the holding cells.

"Steve?" I asked tentatively.

He was sitting on the bed/bench with his back against the wall and his head hung limply on his chest. I tapped lightly on the bars, and he jerked up quickly. I jumped back in fright, and he looked at me with blank eyes.

"Steve?" I asked again.

He grunted at me and crossed his arms over his chest.

"I'm here to talk to you about Layla," I said.

He scoffed. "Why? Didn't you hear that I killed her?"

CHAPTER SEVEN

I froze. Steve's words paralyzed me, and I wanted to scream. However, he averted his eyes, and I could tell that he was deeply affected by what he had said. This wasn't a man who was taunting me. He looked broken and impossibly sad.

"Did you kill her?" I asked tentatively.

He looked at me in surprise and shook his head profusely. I knew that I was probably being naïve, but a wave of relief washed over me. I believed him.

"Okay," I said, nodding quickly, "okay, we can work with that."

"No, we can't," Steve said, shaking his head at me. "The police think that I did it, which means that I'm done for. They've got their guy. Everything is stacked against me, and they caught me trying to leave town. That's as good as confession in their books. Everyone is going to believe that the homeless guy killed the pretty librarian. It's a good story. It all fits and it all makes sense, so they won't look any further."

My heart broke for him, and I took a step closer. He was right. It was a neat and fitting conclusion. People would rather believe that the dirty stranger killed Layla instead of one of their own. Otherwise, they would have to live with the knowledge that one of their neighbors or friends was a murderer. It was a scary truth to acknowledge.

"Why were you at the library that night, Steve?" I asked carefully.

"Layla was helping me," Steve said with a sigh.

That sounded like Layla, and I found myself smiling slightly. It hurt to think that she might have been murdered by someone that she was trying to help. While I doubted that Steve was the murderer, I couldn't dismiss the possibility either. Sterling might've had more evidence than he'd revealed to me. It made sense, because it was unlikely that he would disclose all the information about the case, especially to a nosy civilian.

"How was she helping you?" I asked, looking over my shoulder to make sure that no one was coming.

"She would give me food, clothes, toiletries...stuff like that. It was embarrassing, but I needed a little help, and she always made sure to keep some practical stuff for me. I had a job—a small one at a farm in the next town over—and she offered to give me some old clothes and let me use the shower at the library. She said that this job might lead to others. Sometimes, she would let me do odd jobs around the library. It wasn't steady because they were having some problems with the budget, but it was better than nothing."

I nodded slowly.

"I went there that day, but I couldn't get hold of her. I knocked and knocked and called, but no one came to the door. She had never dropped me before, and I was quite worried about her. When I checked the door, it was locked. Look, I thought about trying to get in; I'm handy with locks, but how would that look? Something felt off to me, and I just knew that something was wrong, but I didn't know what to do. I decided to leave and try again the next morning."

"That's why you were at the library," I surmised. "But why did you run?"

"I was late for my job," Steve said, sounding some-what teary as he ran his hands through his hair. "I real-ized I was late, so I decided to run to catch the bus. Someone on the bus heard about the murder and called the police. They said that I was trying to leave town. Everyone knew that Layla always helped me."

I shook my head sadly. "Didn't the police corroborate your story?" I asked in shock.

"Apparently, no one at the farm wanted to talk to the police." Steve let out a long sigh. "To be honest, I don't think they tried very hard to confirm my story. Since they couldn't get an answer, they simply assumed that I was lying and that was it. Now they have cause to keep me, and it's only a matter of time until they build a case against me. There's literally nothing I can do about it."

It made sense, and I felt terribly sad for him. Layla would have hated all of this. She believed the best of Steve, and now he was being turned into her murderer. I didn't know what to believe, but the thought of an innocent man going to jail made me want to scream. Especially since it meant that the real murderer would go free.

"Do you know a woman named Kara Meyer?" I asked.

Steve grimaced, and I took that as a yes. It seemed that everyone had the same expression when Kara was mentioned. She certainly wasn't the most pleasant person I had ever dealt with.

"That woman is a nightmare," Steve said. "She was always on Layla's case about something. Apparently, she wouldn't rest until Layla banned the books that she didn't agree with. Layla showed me the list once, and I nearly choked. It had hundreds of books on it. Some of them were just banned because of one or two scenes. Layla said that Kara would have excelled in nineteen-thirties Germany."

I chuckled despite the situation, and he smiled slightly.

"Do you think she could have done something like this?" I asked.

Steve sighed and shrugged. "Look, I've learned the hard way not to judge anyone's appearances. Kara looks like an upstanding lady, but no one really knows what a person is capable of. I don't know if she was mad enough to kill Layla, but maybe it was an accident. Who even knows? I definitely wouldn't rule anything out."

I nodded slowly. He made a lot of sense. It would be a mistake to rule anyone out simply because they didn't look like they were capable of murder. Kara had certainly proven that she was a vindictive person, and she had admitted that she thought that Layla got what she deserved. What kind of normal person would say something like that? Kara also wouldn't be the focus of an investigation, especially if the police had someone like Steve in custody already.

"What about Jason Diggs?" I asked.

Steve's expression soured, and he glared at a spot on the ground.

"If anyone was capable of doing this, then it's that guy," Steve said bitterly. "He's a horrible, horrible man. Do you know they thought about asking him to be the prosecutor for this case? If that happens, then I might as well give up now. He wouldn't rest until I was locked away for good. And you know what? I'd have to sit there and wonder if the lawyer sending me to jail was the same guy who killed Layla."

My eyes widened, and I crossed my arms over my chest. "What did he do to you?"

"He was always at the library," Steve said with a shudder. "It was terrible. When they were dating, I felt like I had to stick around in town just to make sure she was safe. She became this nervous wreck. It was awful."

I looked away quickly and blinked a tear out of my eye. "What happened?" My voice was surprisingly steady, and I was a little proud of that.

"He called her all the time and picked fights about the smallest things. She told me that he once got angry because some guy looked at her at the store. Once they were done fighting, he'd become all loving and sweet again. It was like being on a rollercoaster. One day, I told her that she was in an abusive relationship. She looked at me with this blank expression and started laughing."

"Laughing?" I echoed in surprise.

"Yeah, she told me that she was relieved that I put it that way because she thought she was going crazy. Apparently, things weren't going well with the library... you know, moneywise. She'd been so focused on making sure the library was going okay that she hadn't noticed how much Jason was affecting her. She called him right then and there to tell him that she was done with him."

"How did he react?" I asked, feeling a pit of dread opening up in my stomach.

"He told her that she was making a huge mistake and that he was going to make her regret it. I helped her pick out a can of pepper spray online and made her promise that she wouldn't leave work in the dark anymore."

"That's so scary," I breathed. "And that's when the harassment started?"

"Yeah. I told her to go to the police, but she didn't want to. Apparently, she was afraid that it would become a 'he-said-she-said' situation. Turns out that she was right not to come to these people. Besides, Jason is some big-shot lawyer, and she was just a librarian. You can see why she was hesitant."

Before I could respond, Jasper wandered into the room. He hurried up to me, and I was about to pick him up when he spotted Steve. He stopped short then and shot into the cell toward Steve.

Steve chuckled and picked him up gently. Jasper began purring and butted Steve's chin with his head. I stared at him in shock, and Steve grimaced apologetically.

"Sorry, cats love me for some reason. It's a bummer because I'm allergic to them."

"I'm sorry." I rummaged through my bag and handed him some allergy pills as he attempted to hand Jasper back to me.

Jasper meowed in distress as Steve tried to hand him over. The naughty cat clung to Steve's shirt, causing him to laugh again. I finally managed to wrestle Jasper through the bars, but not before he swiped at me. It wasn't an aggressive action, but rather one of protest. He didn't use his claws and was probably upset that I was trying to wrestle him away from his new friend. However, when I had him in my arms, he settled down and rested his head on my shoulder.

"Sorry, Steve. I should probably head out before anyone catches me in here."

"Be careful," Steve told me with a somber expression. "Don't put yourself in any danger. It's just not worth it, okay? Remember, this person left Layla under that bookcase; they won't hesitate to do it again if they feel that you're getting too close."

I stopped short at his words and looked back at him. No one had shown such concern for my welfare during this entire investigation. It was as if only Steve really understood what I was attempting to do. I nodded slowly and gave him a grateful smile. It seemed hard to believe that the man who cared about my safety was the person who was being accused of such a heinous crime.

Before I left the holding room, I peeked around the corner to make sure that no one would spot me leaving. Thankfully, Aunt Daisy Mae was still keeping watch, and I was able to join her without anyone noticing. The policemen were back at work and all glared at Jasper as we walked past. My heart was beating loudly in my chest, and I was scared that someone would stop us at any second.

Just as we were about to walk through the doors, someone called my name. I turned around and saw Sterling marching up to us with a stormy expression. Aunt Daisy Mae and I looked at each other nervously. He stopped in front of me, and I could feel the rage pouring off him.

"Yes?" I asked innocently.

"Keep that animal on a leash, or don't bring it around here," he growled, pointing an accusing finger at Jasper.

"Yes, sir," I said meekly, nodding profusely. However, Jasper had a different idea and promptly nipped the detective's finger, causing him to cry out in fright. It wasn't a hard bite, but it probably surprised the detective. In Jasper's defense, the detective had been waving his finger rather suggestively in Jasper's face.

CHAPTER EIGHT

The next few days were a flurry of activity as we prepared for Layla's funeral. Layla's parents came through, and it was clear that they weren't able to do anything because of their grief. It was heartbreaking to see them so lost in their pain, and so Aunt Daisy Mae and I began planning the funeral. It wouldn't be a large service, but it would be enough to say goodbye to Layla with dignity, which was something her murderer never afforded her.

The news about Jason and Layla broke out, and people lined up to console the grieving boyfriend, but I couldn't stand to be in the same room as him. No one seemed to notice the tension, and he was decent enough not to bother her parents, but nothing he did would be able to redeem him in my eyes. Even if he hadn't killed

Layla, he'd made her last few months uncomfortable and scary. She had to deal with his constant harassment, and he probably caused her immeasurable distress.

Unfortunately, the news that Steve had been arrested also made its way to the public's ears. Kara seemed to be the champion against Steve and was spreading terrible rumors. When I heard some of the stories, I felt sick to my stomach. Even though most of the facts of the case were well-established, people were letting their imaginations get the best of them. Some people claimed that Steve was part of a Satanic cult and had killed Layla after she refused to join his religion. Others believed that Steve had stalked Layla, and the reason that she had been so jumpy in recent months was because she had been terrified of him. No one wanted to entertain the possibility that Steve was innocent.

Thankfully, due to Jason's connection with Layla, he was disqualified from becoming the prosecutor in the case. It was a small relief, but victories were so far and few in between, that I had to celebrate what I could.

When Ellie arrived two days before the funeral, I fell into her arms and began crying. The pressure was insane, and I felt incredibly guilty for not continuing with the investigation. Time was running out for Steve, but I didn't have enough time to investigate a murder and plan a funeral.

"It's going to be okay," Ellie said soothingly as Jasper settled on her lap.

"I don't see how this is going to be okay," I said in distress. "Steve is most probably innocent, and no one believes that. Kara is turning the public against him, but there's a chance that she might have killed Layla. This is insane, and the police aren't doing a single thing to stop her."

Ellie listened intently, nodding as I spoke. It helped to have someone to rant to. Aunt Daisy Mae spent most of her time helping Layla's parents, and I was left to deal with my emotions alone. Jasper was a huge help. He sensed that something was wrong and kept close to me at all times. It was one of the only things that was keeping me sane.

"Careful, Claudia," Ellie said kindly, "you're doing what Kara's doing right now. You don't know for sure that she's a killer, so you can't go around accusing her. You need to find evidence and then make an accusation like that. You see how easily people are influenced; you don't want to turn into someone like Kara."

I grumbled under my breath, but she was right.

"The funeral will be done soon, and then you'll get right back to the investigation," Ellie reminded me. "Don't take on more than you can handle or else you'll be completely useless. One thing at a time, one day at a time. Just get through this funeral, and allow yourself to grieve for your friend."

I smiled gratefully at her. "What happened to letting the police do their job?" I asked with a wry smile.

"You tried that. Now if anyone asks you why you didn't go to the police, you have a paper trail which proves that you tried to. That way, the police will get in trouble, not you."

"You're a genius," I said, looking at her in amazement. "I didn't even think about that."

"Let me be your brains," Ellie said with a playful wink. "By the way, have you found any suspects besides Jason and Kara?"

"What? Aren't those two enough for you?"

"It's all well and good, but what if neither of them is the murderer? You're so focused on them that you might have developed tunnel vision. Remember, follow the evidence, not your feelings. Look, Jason is a pig, but is he a murderer? Yeah, Kara is a menace, but did she kill Layla?"

"Yeah, that makes sense," I said thoughtfully. "The evidence does seem to point toward them, but maybe I'm missing something."

"Maybe, maybe not. But it's good to keep an open mind."

"Thanks for coming all this way. I don't know what

I'd do without you. Honestly, this whole thing has been driving me completely mad."

"Of course," Ellie said, waving her hand dismissively. "How's your murder board?"

I grimaced. It had been a while since I had checked on that. When Ellie heard that, she shook her head at me, and we quickly began working on it again in the back of the van. As we worked, Jasper jumped in between piles of books. I kept picking him up then putting him down, and he decided to make a game out of it.

Every time, I put him down on the floor, his tail swished around maniacally. As soon as I turned my back, he would jump back onto the shelves, and I would have to chase after him before he knocked something over. Finally, Ellie had enough and went to her own van to make us some coffee. When she got back, I gratefully took the cup from her, but I made a fatal error by turning my back both on Jasper and the murder board.

I realized my mistake when Ellie's eyes widened, and I turned around to see him studying the board. We had updated the board with more pins and strings connecting people to Layla's murder. It looked colorful and must have been an enticing temptation for the cat.

"Jasper," I said, my tone pleading, "please don't..."

However, as soon as I started speaking, Jasper

pounced on the board. He caught some string but wasn't able to keep himself upright and immediately crashed to the floor, taking the board with him. I let out a moan and covered my eyes. When I opened them, Jasper was in the corner of the van, watching the board with massive eyes.

"Well," Ellie said with a sigh, "back to work then. And you wonder why I don't have a cat?"

"You love Jasper," I said, already forgiving him for his act of vandalism.

As we bent down to pick up the various pieces of paper, I found my notes of my interview with Steve. I read through it quickly, and something struck me as I went over his words again.

"Do you know what I just realized?" I said, straightening up thoughtfully.

"That you hate cleaning and would rather leave it all to me?" Ellie grumbled as she continued picking up the pieces of the board.

"No, no," I said. "Steve mentioned that Layla was stressed about work."

"Yeah? So am I. People just don't buy as much coffee as I'd like them to," Ellie said with a shrug.

"No, you don't get it. Layla was so stressed about work, that she barely noticed how Jason was treating her."

Ellie frowned. "That is unusual. She should have noticed that she was in a potentially abusive relationship a long time before Steve pointed it out. She was usually so sensitive to that sort of thing."

"We know her job was the most important thing in the world to her, which means that if something was wrong then she would have been devastated and distracted."

"What exactly did he say was stressing her out so much?"

"Money. He said that there were some budget problems. As far as I know, this library is one of the best-funded public libraries in the county. Besides that, the mayor sponsors some of the programs. His whole campaign included children's literacy. She was so proud of that. What was going on at the library?"

"It's worth checking," Ellie said, leaning against a nearby shelf. "Did she mention anything to you?"

"No, I wish she had. To be honest, we had drifted slightly over the past few months. That happened sometimes. We both had such busy lives, but if I had any idea what she had been going through, I would have made more of an effort. I should have made more of an effort. That's something that's going to haunt me for the rest of my life. What if I had called more? What if I had stopped by unexpectedly?"

"What if pigs could fly? You can't do this to yourself, Claudia. Yeah, you weren't as communicative as you would have liked, but neither was she. That means that she probably understood. She wouldn't blame you, so why should you?"

"I could have been there for her more," I insisted. "She did so much for me, and when she needed me most, I was off living my best life. What kind of friend is that?"

"Is that why you're doing all this?" Ellie asked, holding up the pieces of the murder board she still had in her hand.

I didn't say anything. It made sense if that was the real motivation behind the entire investigation. I had accepted Noah's suggestion so easily, and I expanded on it. Deep down, I knew that he hadn't meant that I should find the murderer on my own. I had turned it into a whole investigation when he had simply meant that I should have kept busy and helped out where I could. However, I was so deep into it now, that the only way out, in my mind, was through uncovering the killer.

"Yeah," I said, running my hand through my hair, "maybe, but if I don't do this, then who will? The police have proven time and again that they aren't going to do it. Sure, Jason or Kara might not be guilty, but someone is. And I'm not willing to believe it's Steve until they find some real evidence."

"I see," Ellie said, looking at me intently.

"I know you probably think I'm taking this too far, but I need to see this through," I said firmly. "Layla deserved better. We all failed her a little. I get that you think that I'm being too hard on myself, but it's the truth. Layla didn't deserve to die alone like that. I will never forget the way I found her. Someone just left her like that, Ellie. They left her behind like she was trash."

"Just another book on a shelf," Ellie murmured under her breath. "Okay, you're right. You need to do this. For Layla."

"For Layla," I agreed.

We smiled at each other, and I was grateful to have her in my life. In all honesty, a part of me had believed that I was in way over my head and that I should have run away after my first encounter with Sterling. Now, I knew I was in way over my head, but I was determined to see things through right to the end. I smiled at Ellie, but that smile quickly disappeared as I heard the sound of claws on the bookshelf. Jasper was back at it again.

CHAPTER NINE

*T*he sun was shining merrily on the day of Layla's funeral, and the streets were busy with people going about their daily lives. It felt wrong somehow, like an insult to Layla's memory that the whole world hadn't stopped for a moment to grieve her passing. I woke up in a foul mood and had to fight the urge to snap at Aunt Daisy Mae for singing in the shower. Jasper must have sensed my mood, because he carefully avoided me all morning.

Just as we were about to leave for the funeral, I noticed Noah's car making its way down to our campsite. My breath caught in my throat, but I reminded myself sternly that we were just friends. I had no business getting so excited to see him. What was wrong with me? I chalked it up to grief.

"Hey," Noah said somberly when he got out of the car. "Sorry I'm late. I had some business to take care of first."

"I forgot my shawl in the tent!" Aunt Daisy Mae announced loudly and randomly, causing us to look at her in surprise. "I will return shortly."

"Return shortly?" I echoed in confusion.

"I think that's your aunt's way of giving us some alone time." Noah chuckled good-naturedly while his words caused me to blush profusely.

"She's kind like that," I murmured, trying to fight through my embarrassment.

Noah's eyes twinkled with amusement, but in a moment, his expression turned deadly serious. He looked at me intently. It felt like he was staring straight into the depths of my being and could read my thoughts. I shook my head at myself. This is what happened when I stayed up late reading. My imagination tended to run wilder than usual.

"How are you doing?" Noah asked, stepping closer to me. I could smell his soap; it had a citrusy scent. He lowered his voice so that Aunt Daisy Mae wouldn't be able to hear him. "Really."

I shrugged, trying to come up with a believable way of saying that I was fine, but I couldn't bring myself to say the words. His brow furrowed worriedly; it was touching but I didn't want to unravel before the funeral. I bit my lip and looked away, but he wasn't about to let me get away that easily.

"Clauds," he said gently, "it's okay. You can tell me."

"Everything is horrible," I said with a watery smile. "Layla is gone, and there's nothing that I can do about it. Even if we find her killer, she'll never come back to us. I don't know what to do with all these…emotions inside of me. There's so much going on, and the only person I want to talk to about all of this is the one person I'll never be able to talk to again."

He let me ramble and listened quietly, nodding slowly to let me know that he was still following me. When I was done, I shook my head and crossed my arms over my chest so that I was hugging myself tightly.

"There's nothing anyone can do to make this better," he said grimly, "but trust me, it gets easier. You'll become strong enough to control the grief."

His tone indicated that he had personally gone through the same process. I looked up at him. My gaze must have held the question that I wasn't brave enough to ask because he shook his head and looked down at his feet.

"Noah?" Ellie's voice interrupted our moment, and for the first time ever I felt a flash of annoyance toward Ellie. It was gone before it could translate into my body language or expression. It would have been nice to have some more time with Noah, but I didn't want to be greedy.

"Ellie!" Noah said with a warm smile. "I didn't know you were here already."

Ellie and Noah had met a few times before, and they got along well. At first, I wondered if they were attracted to each other, but they had developed an almost sibling-like relationship.

A few minutes later, we headed to the funeral which was being held at a local church. The pastor wasn't happy that I had brought Jasper with me, but he didn't say anything about it. The church was endlessly fascinating to Jasper, and he spent most of the service exploring the pews with a curious demeanor, his tail flicking slightly behind him. Most of the town showed up for the funeral, which was touching. However, some of the children got bored and tried to entice Jasper to play with them. Unfortunately, Jasper didn't care for children and hissed whenever one of them got too close.

The service was lovely, and afterwards we all headed to Layla's house where a catering service had set up some finger foods and drinks. We had also set up some pictures of Layla, and soon people were talking about their favorite memories of her.

"Once, I read this book about a kid who fell into a

magical world and had to tame a dragon so that they could leave," one teenager explained, "but I forgot what it was called. I only remembered parts of the plot and what color the book was. I took a chance and asked Layla about it. She found it within minutes. I could barely believe it. She was such an amazing librarian, but it was more than that; she cared about everyone who walked into her library."

Everyone nodded, and a few more looked ready to speak. Unfortunately, a loud crash interrupted the flow of the conversation. Jasper had been exploring the mantle when he pushed over a large vase with a bunch of white flowers. I couldn't tell if it was an accident or not, but he remained on the mantle and looked down at the mess with a bored expression. I quickly apologized and hurried to clean up the mess. By the time I was done, someone else was sharing a story about Layla.

"I don't think I ever met a sweeter soul," an old lady said sadly. "She always stopped whatever she was doing when I came in and asked me how I was doing. I'll miss our little chats; it wasn't much, but it made my days a little brighter."

As they talked about her, I felt myself becoming overwhelmed by emotion. She was everything they said and more.

"She was the best boss I ever had," Melody said tearfully. "We used to put the radio on during quiet moments and just dance while we did our work. She was so much fun; I don't think I'll ever get such an amazing boss ever again."

She buried her face in her hands, and the old lady who'd spoken earlier patted her back comfortingly while tears streamed down her face. Noah, who had been by my side the entire time, squeezed my shoulder gently.

It was a touching moment, but the mood quickly shifted. Some people had angry looks on their faces, and I worried about what would happen next. As if reading my thoughts, someone stepped forward to speak.

"I can't believe that homeless guy killed her," a tall man with a bushy beard said, shaking his head angrily. "She should have never even talked to the guy."

There were a few murmurs of agreement, and I quickly left the room before I said something I would regret. Noah got up to follow me, but I shook my head at him. I needed to be alone.

Layla's house was a modest two-bedroom structure with a quaint garden. Every room had a bookcase, but there were still stacks of books everywhere. She certainly didn't care about separating her home life from her work. As I made my way to her room, I ran my hand over the spines of her book collection. She collected everything from dense scientific journals to trashy romance novels.

Her room consisted of a double bed with a quilt and an armchair by the window. The rest of the room was filled with stacks of books. The ones closest to the bed were the ones she was planning to read soon, while the one she was currently reading would always be stashed under her pillow. I looked over at the pillow and noticed the cover of a book peeking out, but I couldn't bring myself to pick it up. It felt like an invasion of her privacy.

Instead, I sat down on the armchair, with the intention of staring out her window for a little while until I felt well enough to rejoin the others. As soon as I sat down, I jumped up in surprise. There was something under the couch cushion. Of course. Layla was notorious for sticking things under her pillows when she was done with them. I reached under the couch pillow and retrieved her laptop. I stared at it in surprise then, before I could stop myself, eagerly opened it.

She must have been in the middle of using it before leaving for work, because as soon as I touched one of the keys, the screen came to life and there were a few tabs open. I felt like cheering. It was as if Layla had given me one last gift.

I looked through the tabs. It looked like she was

researching the cost of camping equipment and storage units. Strange. I checked her email next, but there was nothing out of the ordinary. One of the emails was linked to her electronic calendar, and I frowned when I read through it. The library was being audited. Maybe that was why Layla had been stressed before she died. I knew from personal experience that audits were never pleasant. I imagined it was worse for government-funded institutions such as libraries.

However, Layla had always been a responsible spender, so I doubted that she'd had much to worry about. I was about to close the window when I noticed that there was something in the drafts folder. It was probably nothing—I had about fifteen drafts that I had just forgotten about—but something moved me to click on it.

When I read my own name, my heart stopped, and I felt a roaring in my ears. I read through the email at lightning speed, but when I was done, I couldn't remember a single word, so I had to go back through the information a second and third time before I comprehended the words.

Dear Claudia,

I've always admired your courage. You always spoke

about opening your bookstore, and when it didn't look like that would happen, you simply found a new way to achieve your dream. While I always admired you, I never envied you because I was living out my own dream. Greenwood Public Library is my life. I know it's not the most exciting job in the world, but it's where I belong. Or, at least, where I belonged.

I remember how devastated you were when your dream of being an editor turned out to be nothing like you expected. You handled it well and found a better dream. Now it's my turn, and I need your help. Soon, I'll be fired from my position as librarian, and I have no idea what I'll do with myself. You're the only person who might understand the loss I'm facing.

This is a lot to ask, so please feel free to say no. I was wondering if I could stay with you for a few weeks until I get back on my feet? I'll bring my own tent (if I ever figure out which one is the best, I'm still comparing prices) and I won't get in the way at all. Let me know.

Love,

Layla

Despite re-reading the email at least a dozen times, I couldn't make sense of her request. Why had she been so worried about the upcoming audit? She was someone who compared prices of every purchase, and she loved Greenwood Library, so I knew she would never do anything to endanger the library's funding.

I had to get access to the library's financial records. Something was very wrong.

CHAPTER TEN

*A*fter the funeral, Noah and I headed over to the library's bookkeeper. When I had returned to the funeral, Noah had seen that something was amiss, and I ended up telling him about what I had found. He helped me locate someone who knew who handled the financial records for the library. By that point, Melody had already left, and I hadn't wanted to bother her with this. She was going through enough already.

The bookkeeper lived a few houses away from Layla, and when we rang the doorbell, it took her about five minutes to get to the door. When the door opened, I was surprised to see an old woman around the age of eighty.

"Hello," I said politely, "I'm looking for Rosalie Cutler?"

"That's me," the woman said with a smile, "but everyone calls me Rose. Rosalie is so old-fashioned."

Noah smiled, and I elbowed him gently, giving him a warning look. He quickly hid his smile, but his eyes betrayed his amusement.

"You're the bookkeeper for Greenwood Library?" I said, ending the sentence like a question and cursed myself. My incredulity was obvious, but Rose's mouth just twisted into an amused smile.

"Yes, dear, I may be old, but my mind is still as sharp as a tack," she said, and I blushed in shame. "Why don't you come in? I assume you're here to talk about that dear girl, Layla. Such a shame what happened to her. When I heard, I couldn't stop crying."

She turned and led us into the house. I noticed she walked with a pronounced limp and clung to her cane. Her knuckles were white from holding the cane so tightly, and when she sat down, her relief from being off her feet was painfully clear. I surmised that she hadn't attended the funeral due to her disability.

Her home was small and practical. I couldn't see into the bedrooms, but the living room was neatly arranged so that she could get around without tripping over anything. She also had a footrest near her armchair and a tray table full of paper, which was probably where she got her work done.

"How long did you work with Layla?" I asked as we sat down.

"Dear, I worked with that library ever since it was opened in the sixties," Rose explained. "I did that place's books for decades. I retired just before Layla became the librarian, but then my grandson swindled me out of my pension fund, and I desperately needed a job. No one wanted to hire an old lady like me, but Layla stepped up and gave me my old job back."

I grimaced at her story, and Noah looked outraged.

"I hope you pressed charges," Noah said, his expression thunderous. "He shouldn't be able to get away with that."

"Have you met the police around here?" Rose asked with a deadpan expression, and I snorted. "Anyway, that's not what's important. Layla helped me when I needed it."

"She was that kind of person," I said with a fond smile.

Rose nodded slowly, and we lapsed into silence as I thought of a way to ask for what I needed. Was it even legal to get access to the library's financial records?

"I'm sorry I can't offer you any tea or coffee," Rose said, "but my knee is acting up again, and I can't get around like I used to."

"No, please," I said, shaking my head profusely, "it

really doesn't matter. Actually, we came here to ask you something. I was wondering if I could get access to the library's financial records. I found something strange on Layla's computer, and it looked like she was worried about the upcoming audit."

"Who wouldn't be?" Rose asked, shaking her head lightly. "Those auditors are like vultures." She reached over and began looking through the papers on her tray table.

"Rose, would you like me to make you a cup of tea or coffee?" Noah asked politely.

Rose looked up in surprise, then nodded. I felt guilty for not offering myself, but also proud of Noah for being so thoughtful. She quickly explained how she liked her tea and told Noah to make whatever we wanted, too. As soon as Noah left, she resumed her search. It took a minute or two, but she finally found the right stack of papers.

"Here," she said, handing the papers to me. "You'll notice that everything is in order, but if I'm missing something, maybe you could let me know."

"I'm sure it's nothing," I said sincerely. "I just want to find out what could have been making her feel so stressed. She thought that she was probably going to get fired."

Rose looked shocked for a second, but then her face

smoothed out. Despite her age, it was obvious that she had been beautiful in her prime. Her light gray hair curled gently around her head, and her face was heavily lined, but her laugh lines were the most prominent. Rose was dressed in a powder blue shirt and loose-fitting slacks. It was clear that she still put a lot of thought into her appearance.

"You know, a few weeks ago, I would have said that Layla would never be fired," Rose said with a sigh. "She was the best librarian this town has ever had."

"What changed?"

"A few days ago, right before her death, actually, she came to see me. I could tell that something was off. She was fidgety and distracted. Not rude, never rude. That girl didn't have a rude bone in her body, but there was something that was bothering her. She asked me for the exact same thing you asked me. Well, I gave her a copy of the records, and she was supposed to return it, but she never came back."

Rose's eyes filled with tears, and she shook her head quickly. I took a box of tissues from a nearby table and handed it to her. She accepted one gratefully, and Noah entered the room with the drinks just as she composed herself.

"Why, thank you, dear," Rose said, gratefully accepting the cup of tea.

I thanked Noah and quickly began paging through the records. Unfortunately, I was absolutely useless with numbers, and my head was swimming before long. Noah must have guessed that I was struggling because he kindly offered to look through it himself. I handed the pages over to him. He did some financial work at his company and would know what to look for. As he read through the pages, his brow furrowed, and he pressed his lips into a thin line.

"What's wrong?" Rose asked worriedly. "Did I miss something?"

"No," Noah said, shaking his head quickly, "you didn't do anything wrong, Rose, but there's something wrong here. There's a lot less money here than there should be. Please don't be offended, but is it possible that you missed anything?"

Rose thought for a moment, then got up with difficulty. She motioned for us to follow her and led us to the guest room. It doubled as an office, and she showed us all the information she had received from the library. Noah and I spent the next few hours poring over the books, and by the time it was dark, we had gone back through years of information.

"Well, what's the verdict?" Rose asked when we were finally done.

Noah sighed and looked at me grimly. "It looks like

money is disappearing out of the library's accounts. It was small amounts at first, but the amounts steadily increased. I tried to account for where it could have gone to, but there's no explanation in the books."

"Do you think someone is stealing from the library?" I asked in shock.

"Either that, or the library has been poorly managed for years."

"Never," Rose said firmly. "Layla was a great manager. Someone is stealing from the library. I'm sorry, but that's the only explanation."

"If someone has been stealing from the library for years, then how did Layla only realize it now?" I asked, feeling a sick pit in my stomach.

"At first, the books looked great," Noah explained, "nothing was wrong, but I only took a longer look because you were so convinced that Layla was worried about the library's finances. That's when I started noticing a pattern of discrepancies. When I went back, I found the larger problems. The upcoming audit probably prompted Layla to take a better look at the finances."

"She probably realized that the discrepancies looked like mismanagement and assumed that she would be fired," I said. "That's horrible. Poor Layla."

"Poor Layla, indeed," Rose said with a sigh.

"Well, who could have had access to the library's funds?" I asked. "If we find the thief, we might find the murderer, too."

Rose grimaced. "Oh, dear, there's quite a few people who could have stolen the money. It's a government account, so over the years, different companies have been involved. You know how difficult bureaucracy can get."

"Is there anyone who might have been capable of doing this?" I asked, feeling a wave of frustration wash over me. "Or any specific companies that seemed suspicious?"

Rose went quiet as she thought about what I had asked, "I'm not quite sure," she admitted. "You never know who could be capable of something like this until after the fact. If I had to guess, I would say that the person who seemed most likely to do something like this would be Kara Meyer."

I froze at her words and looked at Noah in surprise.

"Why would you say that?" I asked carefully.

Rose shrugged and bit the inside of her cheek.

"Don't worry, this won't get back to her," I assured her. "We just want to know why you would think that."

She looked at me carefully and sighed. I felt like I

was pushing her a bit far, but it was hard to back off when it was clear that she could help the investigation. I didn't know how to assure her that we were on her side. For a moment, I wondered if Detective Sterling ever felt like that. He dealt with these situations all the time, and he likely became increasingly jaded over the years. Maybe he didn't even know how he came across.

"Well, Kara's husband's company handled all the library's financials until I took over a few years ago."

"I'm sorry," Noah said, "I thought you said that you did the library's financials for decades?"

"Ah, yes, but like I said, I retired and then my grandson swindled me out of my money. I had to go back to work, but while I was gone, a few different companies and individuals handled the work," Rose explained.

Noah nodded sagely, looking vaguely embarrassed.

"You see, Kara wanted to work for the library," Rose continued, "but Layla made sure that she never got the job. It's entirely possible that Kara somehow got access to the library's accounts from her husband and then allowed her anger to get the better of her. I understand that it's a long shot, but there's such a record of bad blood between the two. I know it's a leap to accuse Kara of this, but if there's anyone who could have done this, it's Kara. Especially since it was framed to look like mismanagement."

"Kara might have been setting Layla up," I surmised with a frown. I wondered what Kara would have done if Layla presented her with the same information.

CHAPTER ELEVEN

"I wish you didn't have to go," I said, feeling miserable as I said goodbye to two of my closest friends. I had no idea what I was going to do without Ellie and Noah.

"I wish I could stay, too," Noah said with a grimace, "but my vacation days are all finished, and I can't risk getting fired. I love the mobile bookshop, but I doubt Aunt Daisy Mae would want to share a space with me."

"Think again, handsome," Aunt Daisy Mae said with a wink, causing Noah to blush slightly. It was cute.

"You know I'd stay if I could," Ellie said, giving me a tight hug, "but I have to get back on the road again. People need their coffee, and I need their money."

"We're just a phone call away," Noah assured me, giving me a hug once Ellie let go. "You've got some good leads on this case, but don't do anything reckless. You have to promise me."

"I promise," I said solemnly. "I won't go chasing murderers on my own."

"I'll be there every step of the way," Aunt Daisy Mae said quickly, looping her arm through mine. At that moment, Jasper wandered out of the van and wound himself around my legs as if proving that he would be there for me, too.

Ellie waved and got into the car before driving away. I watched the car until it was just a tiny speck and felt a strange sadness settle over me.

"Hey," Noah said, biting his lip nervously, "I know you're going to think that I'm being overbearing...but I'm a little worried about you. This whole situation is a lot, and I don't want you to get lost in all of it. If you need anything...anything at all, please promise that you'll call me."

Aunt Daisy Mae wiggled her eyebrows at me before promptly turning around and walking away. Jasper stayed by my feet, looking up at Noah with wide eyes.

"I thought your vacation days were all used up?" I joked, trying to lighten his intense mood.

He smiled slightly, then took a step closer so that he was towering over me. I stayed in place, enjoying his warm, citrusy presence. Noah reached up and brushed a stray piece of hair out of my face, allowing his hand to linger on my cheekbone. The action sent a thrill down my back.

"Promise me," he said in a soft voice.

"If I need you for anything, I'll call you." I closed my eyes despite myself.

His arms drew me in for another, longer hug. It felt right, and I forced myself not to melt into him. I heard Aunt Daisy Mae cheering behind us, and Noah let go of me as if he'd been burnt. After that, he left quickly, and I tried to make sense of the confusing storm of emotions in my heart.

I didn't have long to make sense of it all, because my phone began ringing loudly and rather obnoxiously.

"Hello," I answered with a wistful sigh.

"Claudia!" Melody wailed. "I need your help! The library basement flooded, and there are wet books everywhere. Please, I don't know what to do…"

I winced and moved the phone away from my ear as Aunt Daisy Mae wandered over. Meanwhile, Jasper was distracted by a locust. He flattened himself on the ground and watched it with intense focus as he wiggled his rear end in preparation.

"It's okay, Mel…" I tried to calm her down, but she was blubbering uncontrollably about soggy books which made it impossible to get a word in edgewise.

Jasper finally decided to strike and pounced on the locust. He held his paws over the insect and waited a few seconds before cautiously peeking beneath his paws to see if he was successful. To his clear delight, he had indeed pinned the insect down and promptly picked it up, trotting over to us. He dropped his prize in front of Aunt Daisy Mae and sat down to receive his praise.

Unfortunately, the locust chose that exact moment to attempt its escape and ended up jumping up Aunt Daisy Mae's skirt. Aunt Daisy Mae, predictably, let out a piercing shriek which got Melody to stop her rant. She then ran straight into the van. Jasper ran and hid behind me, completely flabbergasted as to why he didn't get his well-deserved praise.

"Is everything okay over there?" Melody asked with a sniffle.

"Yes, we're fine." I crouched down to scratch Jasper behind his ears. He responded enthusiastically and rolled over to expose his belly. "We'll come over in about half an hour." Which was about how long it would take to coax Aunt Daisy Mae from out of the safety of the van.

It took us well over an hour to get to the library, but I called ahead and got a cleaning service to meet Melody at the library. By the time we got there, a lot of old boxes were packed in the front, while others were being thrown into a dumpster. Melody was directing where everything had to go, and she hardly resembled the crying wreck who had called me earlier.

"Thanks so much for coming!" Melody said, hurrying over to me. "I don't know what I would have done without you. How about you start helping some of the cleaners in the basement."

My eyebrows rose in surprise. I certainly wasn't used to this take-charge version of Melody. However, I had come to help, so I headed down to the basement to begin working. Soon, Melody joined us, mostly to oversee our efforts. When she finally turned her back, I felt free from her eagle-eyed gaze and quickly checked my phone to see if I had any messages. I was disheartened to see that there was no signal down here in the basement. I slid the phone into my pocket and continued working.

It took us several hours to clean up the mess, and by evening most of the basement was clear. As I worked, I got bored and perused through some of the old books. The books that were stored in the basement were mostly outdated manuals and old town records. I opened a box of high school yearbooks from the eighties and began flipping through the pages. It was amusing to see what teenagers thought was cool all those years ago, and I even had some flashbacks of neon tights and teased hair.

As I flipped through the books, I found something surprising. I looked around to make sure that Melody was nowhere to be seen. She had been a real pain all day. When I was sure that she wasn't around, I headed over to Aunt Daisy Mae to show her what I had found. Her mouth dropped open, and she took the book out of my hands.

"Is this what I think it is?" she asked, shaking her head slowly. "I can't believe it."

I shrugged. "It is a small town. I'm sure everyone around here dated each other at some point."

"Still," Aunt Daisy Mae insisted, jabbing her finger at the smiling faces on the glossy page, "this is worth looking at."

We managed to sneak out of the library without Melody catching us and headed down to Jason's office. It was a long shot, but I figured that lawyers worked long hours, and I didn't want to wait a whole day to confront Jason with the information that I had found. Thankfully, his light was still on, and his Lexus was still in the parking lot.

When we knocked insistently on the door, he opened it with a peeved expression.

"What do you want?" he asked abruptly.

"I want to know about your connection to Kara Meyer," I said firmly as I held up the yearbook.

The Yearbook Committee that year had dedicated a whole page to a picture of a young Jason and Kara. Jason had his arms around her, and she was beaming toward the camera. The caption read, "Cutest Couple Ever." Of course, the editor that year had been none other than Kara Meyer.

Jason's expression dropped, and he reached out to take the book from me, but I quickly yanked it back.

"Not so fast," I said, glaring at him. "We know that you two dated. We also know that you and Kara have been spreading false stories about this murder all over town."

Jason scoffed, and Aunt Daisy Mae crossed her arms over her chest angrily.

"And we know that you were at the library on the night she was killed," I said, narrowing my eyes at him. I didn't. It was an educated guess. He had been frequently dropping by the library, and the last call on Layla's phone was from Jason.

My guess hit home because he turned pale and quickly looked around to make sure that no one else was around. I shared a knowing look with Aunt Daisy Mae.

"How did you know that?" he hissed in a low tone.

I put the yearbook in my handbag and kept quiet. There was no way I was going to reveal that I had no hard proof.

"Fine," Jason said, running his hand through his hair in distress, "I dated Kara, but it was just for a few months. That was it! She was way more into me than I was into her. When graduation got closer, I broke it off because there was no way I was going to keep dating her in college. I don't think she ever got over it, though."

"What do you mean?" Aunt Daisy Mae asked with a frown.

"Look," Jason said, leaning against the doorframe, "let's just say that some women struggle to move on. When I got back to town, she definitely hit on me a few times. And when I was dating Layla, she got all creepy. She would come by the office at weird hours and even got into more fights with Layla."

"Okay," I said slowly, "and what about that night at the library?"

"I never went in!" Jason insisted. "I decided that I wanted to see Layla, so I headed over there, but when I called her, there was no answer. Then I saw that Kara was already there, and I left. I didn't feel like dealing with Kara that day."

I didn't quite believe him, but I had gotten him to admit that he was at the library on the day of Layla's murder, and that was more than enough for me. Especially since I had downloaded a voice recorder app on my phone, which meant that his confession was actually worth something.

After we left, I found myself reviewing the interview in my head.

"I don't believe him," I told Aunt Daisy Mae later that night when we got into bed.

"No way," Aunt Daisy Mae said with a huff. "He keeps accusing women of doing the things he did. I think you'll find that Jason probably got too intense for Kara. I don't like the woman, but I like Jason even less."

I snorted at that. It was clear that Aunt Daisy Mae didn't think that impartiality was important during an investigation.

"What if they're both equally bad?" I said thoughtfully.

"What do you mean?"

Jasper made his way over to my bed and promptly jumped onto my knees. He began kneading the blanket and made himself comfortable. It wasn't the most convenient spot for me as it meant that I was pinned down to the bed, but I would never move him.

"I mean, they both had a vendetta against Layla, and they were previously quite close." I stroked Jasper's soft fur. "What if there wasn't just one murderer?"

"Do you think they worked together?"

"I think it's a possibility. Maybe they decided to help each other out. Both of them have been placed at the scene of the crime, so I don't think it's too much of a stretch. Either way, we need proof that Kara was at the library that night."

CHAPTER TWELVE

I didn't sleep well that night as I kept imagining all different scenarios in which Jason and Kara cornered Layla in the library and killed her. My newest theory opened up a lot of possibilities which meant that I only fell asleep in the early hours of the morning. The lack of sleep certainly didn't help my mood, especially since I had to go to the library before it opened to help Melody make sure that the flood didn't make too much of an impact.

"Look what the cat dragged in," Melody said, leaning on the counter as I walked into the library. "What happened? You look finished."

"I didn't sleep well," I said, rubbing my eye as I spoke. "What do you need me to do this morning?"

"Whoa," Melody said, holding up a hand to stop me,

"we can't start work yet. You're exhausted. I know it's not my place to ask this, but are you okay?"

I shrugged and didn't say anything. I didn't want to confide in Melody about the investigation. Especially since she had enough on her plate already.

Melody sighed and lifted herself onto the counter. She crossed her knees and looked at me intently. Her dark eyes cut through me, and I shifted uncomfortably.

"Let's talk," Melody said simply.

"I'm just overwhelmed. Detective Sterling still won't let us leave town, and I need to get on the road to start making some money. My savings aren't great, and it's only a matter of time before I completely run out of money. I know I shouldn't be thinking about that right now, especially since we just had the funeral..."

"I understand," Melody said sympathetically. "Trying to make a living is the worst. When I first started out, I lived on a shoestring budget. It was awful, and I kept telling myself that it would be worth it when I finally made it big."

I thought back to some of the authors I worked with at LionHeart and shuddered. Many first-time authors had been starving artists and were desperate to make any sort of money off their passion. Sometimes that made them easy targets for scam artists. Unfortunately, the publishing house could only take on so many new authors which also meant that the vast majority of authors never got their books onto shelves. It was the worst part of being in the publishing industry, and I was so glad that I didn't have to deal with that anymore.

"I'm glad things worked out for you," I said sincerely. "Thanks for understanding."

Melody smiled. "No problem, and don't worry, I'm sure Detective Sterling will let you leave town soon. I mean, they caught the murderer!"

I went cold and looked at her confusion.

"That homeless guy?" Melody prompted, giving me a strange look. "He was always lurking around here and making me feel uncomfortable. I get that Layla saw the best in everyone, but sometimes I think that she was a little too naïve. He was trouble from the start. I warned her, but she wouldn't listen to me; I sure wish she did because then she would be here with us now."

Melody shook her head mournfully and looked up at the ceiling before looking back at me. I tried to keep my expression neutral, but it scared me that even Melody was willing to accept that Steve was guilty without a shred of reliable evidence.

"Let's get started with all this work," I said stiffly.

Melody must have sensed her mistake and meekly nodded. We worked in silence for a while as we tried to sort through the leftover books that had been brought up from the basement the previous day. Most of the books ended up in the recycling bins, mostly because we didn't see the need to keep them in storage anymore.

"Maybe this was a blessing in disguise." Melody sighed. "Layla always wanted to turn the basement into a rec room, and now we have the space to do it. Maybe we could name the rec room in her honor?"

"That would be nice," I said with a small smile.

When we were done, I began walking back to the campsite. Melody offered to drive me in her shiny red car, but I needed the time to think and clear my head. As I was walking, I noticed the back of the café I had visited a few days before. I stopped short. There was a convenience store and gas station attached to the back, and someone had installed a camera on one of the pillars. It was facing away from the library, but probably had a clear view of the road and sidewalk leading up to the library.

I hesitated, then propelled myself forward. There was only one way to find out if my hunch was correct. The convenience store was occupied by one worker in a neon green polyester shirt with the name of the store emblazoned on the front. He was a skinny, pale young man with sickly white skin who was staring intently at his phone.

Thankfully, there were no other customers in the

store. I grabbed the nearest item on one of the shelves, which happened to be a tube of Chapstick. He didn't look up when I put it on the counter, so I cleared my throat meaningfully.

"Hi," he said, looking up lazily. "Will this be all?"

"Uh, actually..."—I quickly checked his name tag—"Shaun, I need your help. There's a security camera outside, and I was wondering if you could show me some footage from a few days ago."

Shaun snorted and leaned back on the barstool he was occupying. "Do you realize how strange that sounds? What do you want to do with that footage?"

I hesitated. "Well, I can't exactly tell you, but I promise it's nothing bad. I just...need some information."

Shaun chewed the inside of his cheek as he studied me. I held my breath in anticipation, then he shook his head slowly.

"No, sorry, can't do it. I don't know you, and promises don't usually mean anything."

"Look, I need to watch that footage, so we need to work out some sort of deal, because I'm not leaving here."

"How about this," Shaun said, rubbing his chin, "why don't you tell me what you want to do with that information, and we can go from there."

"Okay." I sighed. "Do you know Layla Johnson?"

"Hold on," Shaun said, holding up his hands, "you want to see who went to the library that day?"

"How did you know?"

"Okay, here's the thing…" Shaun looked around cautiously. "Layla was the best. She was always so nice when she came in here. When I heard about what happened, I told the police about the camera, but they said it probably wasn't relevant."

I clenched my hands into fists and shook my head in annoyance. "It might be very relevant. Please let me see that footage? I know I'm a stranger and all that, but I just want to see who was at the library that day."

Shaun hesitated, then nodded quickly. He let me into the back room and showed me how the camera system worked. It was outdated and only showed black and white footage on a small TV screen, but we had a clear view of the street leading up to the library. We saw people traveling up and down the street during the day before we'd found Layla. It was eerie spotting Layla head to work that day.

"What I'd give to be able to warn her not to go to work that day," Shaun said sadly. He was standing at the door, keeping an eye on the shop just in case anyone came in.

I nodded in agreement and tried not to think about it too much.

On the screen, I spotted Melody's shiny new car leaving the library later that afternoon. I waited impatiently for what I knew was coming next. Kara's old Cadillac drove up the street. About half an hour later, Jason's Lexus drove past. Steve walked up the road, and I remembered what he'd told me. By the time he got to the library, the door was locked, and he couldn't get hold of her. Which led me to believe that she was already dead by the time he left. About ten minutes later, Steve walked back down the street. I couldn't see his face, but from the way his shoulders were slumped, I could tell that he was dejected.

I waited for Kara's car. Jason's story checked out, and so did Steve's, but so far Kara was the only one who still seemed suspicious. Five minutes passed, then ten, and finally twenty minutes passed before Kara's car drove past the camera.

"Hold on," I said, pausing the footage. "Did you see how fast she was driving?"

"Yeah." Shaun's eyes were wide. "That was way over the speed limit. If I didn't know any better, I'd say that she was trying to get away from something."

"It looks like it," I said grimly. "Do you think I could get a copy of this video? It might come in handy later."

Shaun nodded and hurried over to help me. It wasn't long before I made my way back to the van where Aunt Daisy Mae was painting and Jasper was lying on a sunny patch and licking his paws contentedly.

"How was your outing?" Aunt Daisy Mae asked, her eyes still trained on her painting.

"I might have found something," I said, trying to contain my excitement. "Kara was definitely the last person to leave the library that night. I think we can place her at the library at the time of the murder, which might be just enough evidence for the police to finally take this seriously."

"It's about time!" Aunt Daisy Mae said. "By the way, someone dropped off a package for you earlier. I wasn't around because I was taking a walk around the neighborhood looking for my muse."

"Thanks." I ducked into the tent. There was a simple brown box on my bed with my name written on the front. When I picked it up from the bottom, my hand came away red and wet. I gasped and dropped the box which fell with a heavy thud.

Aunt Daisy Mae must have sensed that something was wrong because she hurried into the tent. When she saw my hands, she went as pale as a sheet.

"Is that blood?" she asked, looking at the mess on my bed.

"No," I said numbly, smelling it quickly. "It's just red paint. I don't know why anyone would do this."

We both looked at the box in horror. She moved to open it, but I shook my head at her and quickly knelt next to it. I opened it gingerly, as if it was a bomb. Someone had put a book in the box and drenched it in red paint. I opened the front page, and someone had scribbled a message on the page.

Back off!

"Why would anyone do this?" Aunt Daisy Mae asked, covering her mouth with her hands. "Are they trying to threaten us?"

"Yes, I'd say so." I shook my head slowly. "I can't believe this happened."

"Should we take it to the police?" She pulled her cardigan tighter around her body.

"No, but we'll put it in a plastic bag in the fridge to preserve the evidence. Don't worry, Aunt Daisy Mae, this is a good thing."

"How could you say that?"

"It means we're getting close to finding the murderer," I said with a grim sense of satisfaction. I was ready to see this to the end.

CHAPTER THIRTEEN

e headed over to Kara's house as soon as we put the box in the fridge. While I was happy that we were finally getting somewhere in the investigation, I didn't want to delay the process any more than was necessary.

When Kara opened the door, she was surprised to see us and crossed her arms over her chest defensively. She was wearing a navy-blue shirt with khaki pants and sandals, and it looked like she had been working in the garden.

"I would love to chat, but I have a lot to do today," Kara said with a sneer, making it clear that she would rather not talk to us.

"Oh, I think you're going to want to talk to us," I said firmly. "Where were you this morning?"

Kara snorted and pulled the door closer to herself so that we knew she wasn't going to invite us inside. "I don't see how that has anything to do with you," she said primly. "I certainly don't have to explain my whereabouts to the likes of you. We don't live in a police state."

"Are you sure? What do you think they do to books they don't like in a police state?"

Kara flinched and glared at me. She must have hoped that her rude actions would cause us to leave, but rather it made us more determined to stick around and find out what we needed to know. When she saw that we had no intention of leaving, she decided to take things to the next level.

"You better get out of here before I call the cops on you. You're trespassing on private property. I don't want you around here anymore, and if you keep harassing me then I'll have to file a restraining order."

She punctuated her threat by reaching for her phone in her pocket. Once she had it out, she waved it in front of our faces to make her point. I tilted my head slightly at her and studied her intently which caught her by surprise. She took an uneasy step back and looked at Aunt Daisy Mae, who also crossed her arms over her chest.

"I'd rethink that if I were you," Aunt Daisy Mae said, raising her eyebrow.

"Why?" Kara challenged, narrowing her eyes at Aunt Daisy Mae.

"No, wait," I said thoughtfully. "Let her call the police, then we could all sit down and talk about a few things. It might save us a trip if they come here."

"You're right," Aunt Daisy Mae said. "You know what? I think you should go ahead and call the cops. We'll make ourselves comfortable on her porch until they arrive."

Aunt Daisy Mae turned and sat on the stairs of the porch before motioning for me to do the same. Kara's eyes were wide, and she looked at her phone uncertainly.

"What do you want to talk about?" Kara finally relented, her shoulders slumping forward in defeat.

"We know the real reason you hated Layla," I said, as Aunt Daisy Mae got up from the porch steps and shook her skirt lightly to get rid of any dirt.

"I already told you..." Kara started, but I gave her a stern look, and she quickly closed her mouth.

"You were angry because she was dating Jason," I said. "You didn't approve of their relationship and decided to take things out on her."

Kara's mouth twisted slightly, but she kept quiet.

"We know you were the last person to leave the library that day," I continued, and my words caused Kara to flinch then turn pale. "Which means you were very likely the last person who saw Layla alive."

"You can't prove that," Kara said, her voice rising. "That's a baseless accusation, and I could sue you for defamation of character. My cousin is a lawyer, so I could do it easily."

"That's only if your cousin would be willing to represent you," Aunt Daisy Mae said reasonably. "Maybe they won't want to defend you. Unless...is Jason your cousin? That's disgusting."

"No," Kara said, shaking her head profusely. "He's not..."

"We have a video of the street leading up to the library," I interjected before we got too far off track. "It clearly shows that you were the last person to leave the library. We have proof, Kara; you can't get out of this one."

"Don't say that," Kara said miserably. "Please don't say that. The police won't understand... They'll think that I had something to do with the murder. You saw how quickly they arrested Steve; it won't take much to make them change their minds."

"Maybe I would feel kinder if you hadn't run around slandering Steve," I pointed out, and she shrank back in shame.

"I get it." Kara covered her face with her hands. "I

messed up. I didn't mean to... Look, I'm sorry. I have a family...you have to understand."

"I don't think there's anything you could say that would make us understand," I said coldly, narrowing my eyes at her.

"I know," Kara said, shaking her head forlornly. "Layla was your friend. I wouldn't expect you to forgive me. I'm so sorry, please know that I never meant to... I thought that if I did my part to make sure that everyone knew Steve is guilty then that could make up for—"

"Wait," I said, holding up my hand to stop her, "what?"

"What?" Kara asked, taking her hands away from her face and looking at us in surprise.

"What are you talking about?" I asked.

"What are *you* talking about?" Kara echoed, fidgeting with her phone.

"You killed Layla. That's what I thought you were confessing."

"Are you insane?" Kara asked, aghast. "I never killed her."

"Then what were you talking about?" Aunt Daisy Mae asked, scratching the back of her head in confusion.

"I messed with the pipes," Kara said, looking bewildered. "That's why I went to the library that day. I went after they closed and snuck into the basement. I rigged the place to flood because I knew Layla kept some of the books that I wanted to ban in the basement. I figured that if she wouldn't ban the books, then I had to take matters into my own hands."

"You are a terrorist," Aunt Daisy Mae said angrily.

Kara gasped.

"Think about it," Aunt Daisy Mae insisted. "You gave her a list of demands, and when she wouldn't give in, you caused harm intended to force her to give in to your demands. Do you know what that's called? A terrorist!"

"How dare you?" Kara sneered, glaring daggers at Aunt Daisy Mae.

"No, no, enough," I said in annoyance. "So you snuck into the library and messed with the water pipes. What happened next?"

Kara shrugged then sighed. "Layla caught me and threw me out. She said that she was going to ban me for life. Of course, I took offense, and we ended up in a screaming match. I was surprised because she had been angry with me before, but this was a new level of anger. Look…" She lifted up her pants slightly to show off an angry blue bruise. "She literally threw me out of the building. I was shocked. I told her that I would press charges."

Aunt Daisy Mae and I looked at each other in

surprise. I couldn't imagine that Layla would ever do anything violent and guessed that she must have tried to get Kara out of the library and that Kara resisted. I wasn't sure if I believed Kara's story, but her reaction seemed completely sincere. This left me with a serious dilemma because now I was out of suspects, and I had no idea who could have murdered Layla.

"Did you notice anything strange that day?" Aunt Daisy Mae asked, looking at me with a questioning glance.

I could tell that she was also wondering whether or not we could believe Kara.

"Oh, yeah," Kara said. "While I was down there, I heard her screaming at someone. They must have been having an argument or something, because a few minutes later, I heard someone slamming the door. Layla then went quiet for a while, but when she found me, her eyes were all puffy and red. I think she had been crying."

"Do you know who she was fighting with?" I asked carefully.

"No clue," Kara said simply. "By the time I got up there, no one else was around."

"What about Jason?" Aunt Daisy Mae asked.

"No," Kara said. "I looked through the window and

saw him driving past. He never even stopped at the library that day."

"Besides, I don't think she cared enough about him to cry like that," I said. "She must have been really hurt by the argument if it drove her to tears, which means that it must have been someone that she trusted. Maybe one of her friends?"

"Maybe." Kara shrugged. "Oh, and one more thing. I think someone was coming in through the back door when Layla was escorting me out. I wasn't sure, because we were making a lot of noise, but I definitely heard the door open and close. You know, the library echoes."

My heart stopped in my chest.

"Is it possible to access the back entrance of the library without driving past the front?" I asked.

"Yeah. It's not the most convenient route, but it's possible, I guess. Look, I'd love to talk about this more," Kara said sarcastically, "but if you're done, then leave. I don't want you on my porch for any longer than necessary."

I rolled my eyes at her but turned to leave. There was no point in staying anyway. As we turned to leave, Kara frowned.

"Wait," she said with a huff. "One more thing. You assumed that I hated Layla because she dated Jason;

that's not true. And she wasn't the saint that everyone made her out to be either."

I clenched my jaw and looked away from her.

"You better have a good reason for saying that," Aunt Daisy Mae said sternly.

"I do! I wanted that job at the library. Melody's job. We were both up for the position, and I had more qualifications. Besides…I needed the job. We weren't doing great financially either…my husband and I. Then, out of nowhere, Melody got the job. I approached Layla and asked if she could find a place for me at the library. I didn't mind working anywhere."

I frowned. This story sounded out of character for both Layla and Kara, but Kara was finally opening up, and the sincerity of her expression made me hear her out.

"She told me that there wasn't enough money in the budget and that the assistant position was a low-paying job." Kara snorted.

"I'm sorry that you lost out on the job, but those reasons sound perfectly reasonable," I pointed out. "How could Layla hire you if she didn't have any money?"

"That's just the thing," Kara said bitterly. "There was more than enough money. She just didn't want me to get the job, so she lied. Layla was a liar and a vindictive individual. At that point, we had done nothing to each other, and I had gone to her with a sincere request for help."

"How do you know she was lying?" I asked in confusion.

"It's simple. That assistant of hers has been living the high life. About two months after she got the job, she moved into an expensive part of town. Just a few months ago, she bought that expensive car. Obviously, there was more than enough money in the budget for two assistants, but Layla preferred to play favorites."

"What if there wasn't enough money in the budget?" I asked, my eyes widening.

"How would you explain Melody's luxurious lifestyle then?" Kara asked in annoyance.

"It's simple," I said grimly. "Theft."

CHAPTER FOURTEEN

*B*efore I went to the library, Aunt Daisy Mae and I decided to split up to cover more ground. As I drove up to the library, I felt a feeling of dread settle in my stomach. Melody was still in the library, but she looked frantic as I walked in. I quickly checked my phone. There were only two bars of signal, which wasn't great, but it would have to do.

"Claudia," Melody said, looking around worriedly, "can I help you with something?" She pushed her hands into her pockets, and I fought the urge to raise my eyebrows at her.

"We need to talk, Melody." I closed the door behind me.

There was no one else in the library which meant that we could talk in private. I was grateful for that because I was worried that we would have to go somewhere to make sure that no one heard us.

"Can this wait?" Melody asked as she ran a hand through her hair.

I spotted speckles of red on her fingernails, and my expression darkened. She realized what she had done and quickly put her hand back in her pocket. Perhaps red paint was harder to wash off her hands than she had expected.

"I'm a little busy right now," she said.

I shook my head at her. There was a strange smell in the library that I couldn't quite place. It bothered me, but I forced myself to focus on the matter at hand.

"No," I said firmly, "this can't wait. Tell me about that last night. The night that Layla was murdered."

Melody's eyes widened, and she took a step back.

"Tell me the truth," I demanded.

"What do you mean?" Melody asked with a nervous chuckle. "I left early. You know that. I had a gig. And I only arrived after you the next morning. Anyone can tell you; I'm sure a few people saw me leave. I think Jason was right behind me when I left…"

"Yes, but what about the back entrance?" I asked.

Melody grimaced and let out a heavy sigh. It was clear that she knew what was going on. There was no way she could play dumb anymore.

"You just couldn't let it go, could you?" she asked, her eyes narrowing at me. She spat the words at me, as if she wanted to hurt me.

I'd never seen such malice before, and it changed her whole face. She turned from a pretty singer into a monster.

"She found out that you were stealing money from the library," I surmised, gathering all the courage I had. I needed to see this through to the end. "How?"

"She snooped around and found the password to my account," Melody said bitterly. "Everything would have been fine if she just minded her own business. I'm going to be a famous singer; I would have bought her own library if she wanted. Besides, I was only borrowing the money until I could pay it back. It's only a matter of time before I get discovered."

"Stealing is stealing, and what were you planning to do about the upcoming audit?"

"Oh," Melody said dismissively, "nothing. I'm just an assistant. No one was going to suspect me. Besides, Layla always handled that sort of thing."

"She was going to get fired!" I said, my words coming out in a shout. "Layla loved this library. You framed her, you made it look like she was mismanaging this place, but nothing could be further from the truth."

"To be fair, it did take her a while to figure out that money was disappearing," Melody said with a shrug.

"You're the thief! Stop trying to pin this on her. She confronted you that day, didn't she? You two argued, and you stormed off, then she found out that Kara was in the basement."

"What?" Melody asked in shock, looking around frantically.

"She saw you come in through the back door," I lied smoothly. It was better that Melody thought we had more evidence than we did. "And she left. You caught Layla by surprise and killed her, didn't you?!"

"Well, I didn't mean to," Melody said with a little shrug.

I gasped despite myself. While I suspected that Melody was the murderer, it hadn't fully been confirmed. There had been a niggling feeling of doubt in the back of my head, and now there was nothing. Melody killed Layla.

"You killed her," I said, shaking my head and backing away slightly. "She never saw it coming...even after everything."

"I just wanted to talk." Melody sighed. "But she was hysterical. She kept pushing me and telling me to leave. All she had to do was hear me out, then we could have come to an understanding."

"You violated her trust!" I pointed out. "She gave you everything, and you stole from her. You were going to let her be fired!"

"I would have helped her get another job when I became famous," Melody said, waving her hand dismissively. "Besides, it's so much better working for a star anyway."

"She loved this job," I spat, my eyes filling up with tears.

"Whatever. Anyway, she wouldn't stop, so I pushed her back. She must have hit her head or something, because she didn't get back up. It was an accident anyway, so I just turned the bookcase over her so that it would look like more of an accident."

"If you pushed over the bookcase, why didn't they find your fingerprints?" I asked.

"Gloves," Melody said, wiggling her fingers in front of me. Some of the paint flecks caught in the light, and I felt sick.

"If it was an accident, why were you wearing gloves?"

"It was a happy coincidence," she said, and I knew that she was lying. She had planned to kill Layla and wore the gloves to cover up her tracks. Melody wasn't even trying to hide the fact that she was lying and smirked as she said the words.

"You're a monster," I spat, fumbling for the door handle. "You won't get away with this!"

I went to get my phone, but Melody moved so quickly that she was behind me before I knew it. Something sharp pierced my back, and I froze.

"Nothing is going to keep me from achieving my dream," Melody hissed. "You're not going to tell anyone what I told you."

"You've got a knife," I said numbly, my entire body ice-cold with fear.

"So clever," Melody mocked with a laugh. "It's a shame that you couldn't figure it out earlier. Maybe then you would have caught me. Oh well... Come on, let's go."

"Where are we going?" I asked as she steered me away from the door.

"So many questions." Melody sighed. "It's getting annoying; just shut up and wait and see."

I did as she asked and prayed that Aunt Daisy Mae had been able to convince the police to meet us here. However, given their track record, it was safer to assume that I was on my own.

Melody led me down to the basement. The strange smell from earlier was overpowering, and my eyes watered.

I surreptitiously glanced down at my phone, and my

MURDER IN THE LIBRARY

heart sank at the realization that there was no signal down here. Melody probably knew that there was no signal in the basement, which was why she didn't attempt to take my phone from me.

Knife still pressed to my back, she led me through a doorway. The acrid fumes grew stronger, causing my eyes to water even more.

"Oh, that would be the kerosene," Melody said. "Unfortunately, you've proven to be a real problem, and I need to get rid of any leftover evidence. So, I'll be locking you in here then setting this place on fire. Thank goodness you found out about all of this in time, because now I can frame you for the fire, and I'll be long gone in no time. I think it's time for me to head to L.A. or maybe New York. I haven't made up my mind yet, but I'm going to make all my dreams come true."

"You don't deserve any of it," I said angrily, frantically looking around for a window. There was only one at the end of the room, and it was too small for me to fit through. I felt like screaming.

"Yeah, well," Melody said with a shrug. "See you around, or not…"

With that, Melody slammed the door shut. I quickly ran over to the window, but it was nailed shut. I took my shoe off and used the heel to break the window. While I couldn't climb out, I began shouting for help. I knew Shaun was probably still at the store, and I hoped that he wasn't wearing headphones.

Within a few seconds, I smelled smoke and heard Melody's car drive away. I shouted louder and began banging on the pipes. Nothing. I frantically took my phone out of my pocket and tried holding it up to get signal, but it was useless. My phone remained stubbornly unable to connect to the outside world. The smoke was quickly becoming thicker, and I could feel the flames heating up on the next floor. Soon, the whole library would be engulfed in flames, destroying everything that Layla had loved about the place, taking me with it.

My voice was becoming hoarse from screaming. However, I soon saw a strange sight. Jasper was running toward me at full sprint. He jumped through the window and quickly burrowed himself in my arms when I picked him up.

"Am I hallucinating?" I asked out loud.

Jasper answered by purring louder as he clung to my arm. A few seconds later, I caught sight of Aunt Daisy Mae's colorful skirt.

"Claudia?" she called, crouching down by the window.

"I'm here!" I cried out, as a wave of relief hit me. "Please, get me out! The window is too small."

"It's okay, the firemen are here," Aunt Daisy Mae assured me.

"Please get us out!" I called, tears running down my face.

"We're coming, miss," a fireman called as he escorted Aunt Daisy Mae away from the fire.

It took the firemen about an hour to get through the door. Apparently, Melody had set the fire right in front of the basement door, which meant that it was especially difficult to get through the door. During the entire ordeal, Jasper clung to me. When the smoke got thick, he pressed his head against my chest, and I crouched low so that we wouldn't get the brunt of the smoke.

Meanwhile, Aunt Daisy Mae sat by the open window and spoke to me, even though the firemen kept trying to get her to a safe distance. Her support meant the world to me, and I knew that I would fall apart without her.

I told her about Melody's actions and gave her my phone which had been recording the whole time. She took it to the police and quickly returned so that I wouldn't be alone anymore. While I knew that she had to go to the police, I hated it when she was gone. Without her there, I was faced with the terrifying reality of my situation.

Jasper's presence also helped, and I felt infinitely less alone than I had before. My mind grappled with the situation I found myself in, and I wasn't sure if the firemen would get me out in time. I wondered if Layla had felt the same in her last moments, and a fresh surge of grief hit me. There had been no one to save her.

Finally, the firemen reached me and draped a blanket over my shoulders before escorting me out of the building. To my surprise, there were a myriad of vehicles outside. Detective Sterling and the Fire Marshal were busy directing everything, and when Sterling saw me, his face crumpled in relief.

I knew it wasn't his fault, but I couldn't help but blame him. I would never have had to face Melody alone if he had taken me seriously from the beginning. Aunt Daisy Mae rushed over to me and went with me to the ambulance which was waiting nearby.

Detective Sterling walked over with a conflicted expression on his face, but I turned my head away from him.

"Claudia..." he started, but I looked over at him angrily.

"Do you believe me now, Detective?"

CHAPTER FIFTEEN

*P*acking up the van was an interesting exercise. Everything had its space, and it took us about half an hour to pack everything up. I thought that it would be one of the worst parts of being on the road, but there was something therapeutic about packing everything in its place and heading to our next destination.

I loved it.

"Do you think we'll come back to Greenwood anytime soon?" Aunt Daisy Mae asked, looking around the campsite that had been our home for the past few weeks.

"Hopefully not," I said with a chuckle.

My throat still hurt from my ordeal in the library, but the doctors had cleared me and declared that I was able to leave the hospital without any problems. It was a relief. The vet also cleared Jasper, who seemed to be back in good spirits. I bought him a shiny new toy at the pet store. It was a fluffy mouse with a bell inside and sparkly paper in between its fur. The shop's assistant assured me that it was a popular toy. Of course, Jasper had no interest in the toy and spent most of the morning playing with the paper bag that it came in.

I had a hundred pictures of him peeking out over the top of the bag with wide eyes. It was adorable. He was my hero, and I was determined to keep spoiling him for the rest of his life. It turned out that when the police wouldn't listen to Aunt Daisy Mae, she returned to the campsite to pick up the threat that Melody had left behind. Jasper insisted on climbing in the van with her and wouldn't leave her side until they got to the library.

Aunt Daisy Mae had been on her way to the police station when she saw smoke rising from the library and headed over to the Fire Department instead. That decision likely saved my life, and I also bought her a thank-you gift. She loved her new paints and had finally finished the painting she had started when she first arrived.

"You know, it's the person who was bad, not the place," Aunt Daisy Mae pointed out. "Who knows? You might even find that you miss Greenwood after a while. Sure, it might be a long while, but I think you'll miss it."

"I'll miss Layla," I said firmly.

"Yes, and Layla loved this place. Sometimes when we don't have our loved ones anymore, it helps to go to the places they loved. It helps you feel connected to them."

"Sure, Aunt Daisy Mae," I said, but we both knew that I didn't believe her. I was convinced that I would never set foot in Greenwood again.

"Besides, the danger is all gone. They arrested that terrible girl, and she'll be in jail for a long time. You won't ever have to see her again, besides the trial," Aunt Daisy Mae said.

"That won't be for a long while though," Noah assured me as he came back for another load to put in the van.

I gave him a grateful smile, and he winked at me. He had arrived as soon as he heard about my ordeal. I wasn't sure what deal he had made with his boss, but he had been with us for the past two days. His help was invaluable, and I felt safer with him around. Hopefully I would start feeling like myself again once we were on the road.

Even though I wasn't hurt by the fire, I kept having nightmares about being caught in a blazing inferno. I also got frights more easily and struggled to go anywhere on my own. Thankfully, Jasper insisted on going everywhere with me, and his presence soothed my anxiety.

The police had caught Melody just a few hours after she tried to get away. She had been so sure that people would be distracted by the fire that she hadn't tried too hard to hide her tracks. Melody confessed to the murder after about an hour of interrogation.

In recognition of all my efforts in the investigation, the Greenwood police station issued a formal letter of apology to me, which I promptly tore up and threw in the trash. I never wanted them to apologize; I only ever wanted them to find Layla's murderer, and they weren't able to do that. Detective Sterling tried talking to me a few times, but I always rebuffed his efforts. I wasn't in a forgiving mood yet.

"So, where to next?" Noah asked. "Wherever the wind blows?"

"Something like that," I said in amusement. "We're heading to a book market in the next county. It should be a very interesting trip."

"Hopefully it won't be as eventful as this trip," Noah said, shaking his head slowly.

"You know, you're welcome to join us," Aunt Daisy Mae said, wiggling her eyebrows suggestively. "There's plenty of space in the tent."

"Thanks for the offer," he said with a chuckle, "but I think I'm going to have to pass for now. I need to get back to work before they fire me. I told them I had a family emergency to take care of, but that's only going to get me so far."

"Thank you for coming," I said, giving him a tight hug.

"Of course," Noah said with a wide grin. "And listen, let me know when you get to your destination. I think I might be able to swing by and say hi. Or maybe...we could go get some dinner sometime. Just you and me."

I looked up at him in surprise. He looked nervous and was biting his lip as he waited for me to answer. Aunt Daisy Mae covered her mouth with her hand to keep from squealing and quickly hurried away to give us privacy, which I appreciated.

"What made you decide to ask now?" I asked in amusement.

"I know it isn't the best time," he said sheepishly, "but...I've been wanting to ask for a while, and it seems like you could do with a distraction, so..."

"You want to be my distraction?" I surmised playfully.

"I don't know if I'd put it like that," Noah said, turning red, "but I think we have fun together, and I'd like to get to know you...better."

"It sounds like a date," I said with a soft smile.

He looked at me in wonder, and I felt myself melt. It had been a while since I felt so excited about a date. Maybe this would be the start of something special.

After that, we packed the van up and were about to head out on the road. I got a call from Ellie, who wanted to make sure that everything was okay. She had been able to come over for a day after the ordeal in the library but had to head back out on the road again. When she found out about my financial situation, she gave me a substantial amount of money which would see us through until we got back on our feet. I tried to argue with her, but she wouldn't allow me to return it. To be honest, the gift was a relief, and it came at exactly the right time.

I said goodbye to Noah and confirmed the details of our date, watching as he drove away. I knew I was going to miss him and found myself bubbling with excitement for our date. Just as we were about to leave, a strange car drove up to our van, and a man in an expensive suit got out.

"Are you Claudia Madison?" he asked.

"That's me," I said, looking at him warily.

He was a tall, handsome man in his late thirties with dark blond hair and brown eyes.

"I'm Mayor Linden," he said, extending his hand for

me to shake. I shook it uncertainly and looked at Aunt Daisy Mae, who was watching the mayor with interest. I guessed it was romantic interest. It always was with Aunt Daisy Mae.

"How can I help you, mayor?" I asked politely.

"Well…" he said with a sigh, "I find myself in a bit of a bind. You see, Layla Johnson was one of the best librarians this town has ever seen. Her absence creates a real void in town, and I was wondering if you could help me with that. You see, I was wondering if you could take over her position."

It was a kind offer, but I recoiled as if he had slapped me. There was something disturbing about taking over Layla's position.

"We're going to renovate the library and reopen it in a few months' time," he explained. "It will have a state-of-the-art computer section, an interactive children's section, and all new books. We were hoping that you could help us with the renovations and buying the books. You see, this was all Layla's dream, and we think it's about time that it becomes a reality."

"Thank you for your kind offer," I started, but he quickly cut me off.

"We also gave Steve a regular job at the library as a handyman, and I think it would help him a lot if he worked for a familiar face. He told us about how you were the only one who believed that he was innocent. That meant a lot to him."

I pressed my lips into a thin line and thought about it. It would be nice to work with Steve, but I still couldn't envision myself filling Layla's shoes. It felt wrong.

"And one more thing," the mayor said. "We will be renaming the library in Layla's honor. It will now be known as the Layla Johnson Public Library. The opening ceremony will take place as soon as the renovations are complete."

"I'll bet Kara is going to love that," I said with a snort.

"Kara Meyer was the one who suggested it," he said with a wry smile.

I looked at Aunt Daisy Mae in surprise, and she shrugged at me.

"We've also warned Jason about his behavior," the mayor said grimly. "We will make sure that he never harasses another woman again."

"Thank you." My voice was thick with tears. "Those are all such thoughtful gestures, and I know Layla would have appreciated them all."

"We couldn't protect her," the mayor said with a sigh, "but we'll do our best to honor her memory."

I nodded in appreciation again, not trusting myself to speak. At that moment, Jasper walked up to Mayor

Linden and turned on his back, purring the whole time. The mayor crouched down and began scratching Jasper's belly, which Jasper adored. The cat then turned onto his stomach suddenly and began playing with the mayor's shoelaces.

While he was preoccupied, I looked over at Aunt Daisy Mae for advice. She smiled gently at me, and I knew she was letting me know that the choice was mine. I smiled back at her and looked over at the mobile bookshop. It represented years of dreaming and all the courage I ever had. If I hadn't gone on the road, I might've never been brave enough to find Layla's killer. Besides, she understood what it was like to be living her dreams. She would never have begrudged me for living my dream.

"So?" Mayor Linden asked when he straightened and looked at me.

"Thank you for the offer," I said sincerely, "but I'm happy where I am. I don't think I'll be settling down anytime soon, but I would like to work for you as a consultant. I can help you design Layla's dream library and source quality books for the community. If you'd like, I can even help you find a new librarian."

Mayor Linden looked disappointed, but he nodded.

"I'll be in touch," he said with a respectful nod, "and I'll see you soon."

"I thought you didn't want to come back here?" Aunt Daisy Mae said once he left.

"I didn't," I said with a chuckle, "but this is a good enough reason to change my mind, I think. Now come on, the road awaits."

# # #

Thank you for reading! Want to help out?

Reviews are crucial for independent authors like me, so if you enjoyed my book, **please consider leaving a review today**.

Thank you!

Penny Brooke

ABOUT THE AUTHOR

Penny Brooke has been reading mysteries for as long as she can remember. When not penning her own stories, she enjoys spending time outdoors with her husband, crocheting, and cozying up with her pups and a good novel. To find out more about her books, visit www.pennybrooke.com

Printed in Great Britain
by Amazon

20775118R00088